TWIN BOSSES

Twin Bosses

A Scorpion Sting

John L. Clark

Dedicated to: The one who never lost faith in me myself, all those who have a dream and would never let it fail, to my family who's been by my side never letting me give up on myself,

Thanks to: God for giving me the ability to continue to create awesome novels after novels. My twin Lenora, sister Josephine, nephews, Lawson, Zahair, and Trayvond, Niece Skye, brothers, Komplete and Dumar, Uncle, Dennis Butcher his loving wife Yvonne Butcher, their children Eunice, Karriem, and Reva, my bestie Shaniqua Laydee Houston, Angie Mack and my boy Bang and all those who support me.

Contents

Growing up without my twin in my life was really fucked up. Don't get me wrong, I had friends and a lot of them but who are they if you couldn't trust them they'll just be a bunch of individuals around you taking up your space. My oldest brother got murdered three days after his 19th birthday, and that just broke my mother's spirit. First my dad dies, then my brother, and when that happened my mother just lost it which had me to move back home. I helped my sister get into college and out of all the bad shit I've been through, the worst thing I ever faced was being separated from my twin when we was eight. And trusting mother fuckers really wasn't happening until I met Blunt, a big time hustler from my neck of the woods, Brooklyn.

Blunt was my baby. I met him on my 17th birthday. When I seen him I was with my girl Melly and he was walking with one of his boys. Now don't get me wrong his boy had style but Blunts swag was on a million. He had a mocha chocolate complexion, curly baby fro, smooth clean shave and some killer green eyes. I didn't have that grown up look in my face but I did have it going on a little something, something in the body. I had my mother's strong check bones, and my dad's full lips, my mom's and my dad's smooth chocolate complexion, I had my mom's looks a little in the face but everybody always said I was a splitting image of my dad. I had my hair going back in two cornbraids which made me look great, my Grandmother's sexy bedroom eyes, and although I was young, I was growing into my woman's body, my thighs was nice and thick and my breast was trying it's best to be noticed. I had on my O-Looche leopard print sweat suit which hugged my body allowing every little curve I had to be noticed, and my matching Nikes. I had that Chase look with an E.B.T life and that Swiss bank feel but have an S.S.I. budget and a bitch needed to get that resort every week life.

When I got with Blunt my life changed. He taught me everything he knew and what he wasn't telling me I learned from my Uncle. I had to move in with my Uncle when my mother lost it when my dad died which wasn't bad at all. When I was with Blunt I felt like a queen and got everything I wanted or needed. He took me everywhere I wanted to go and gave me all I needed. He made me feel like a goddess until one night he was out with his boys in a club when some guys came in and shot up the V.I.P and my Daddy and his boy, Take, got shot up. At that time

Blunt sent me out of town to meet with one of his connects. When I got back to the city, my baby house was crowded with his team yelling and screaming there were women even out there crying and going crazy like they had his kids. When I got out of my car my man's homeboy Blaze, came over letting me know what had happened. When he told me my baby was gone, I felt sick and almost fainted. He also informed me the situation was going to be taken care of when he calmed me down he told me something that I already knew which wasn't a surprise. He looked me long fully in my eyes and said.

"You know my boy loved you right?" he asked then he continued "Well with that being said he left you this" he said displaying a pair of keys.

"And this is to what?" I asked.

"A spot, I'll take you there in the morning," he said giving me a hug and a kiss on the forehead. He said while still holding me, "Go get some rest and me and the family is going to deal with this shit." he let me go and said. "You know I love you sis and as long as I'm alive I got you."

While I was lying in bed I couldn't sleep. Since I'd been with Blunt I fell asleep and woke up beside him. Now I was lying in bed missing my daddy so I got up and went outside. I didn't have any specific place of going so I just got in my car and I just drove. I drove until I got tired so when I came to a stop, it was at my mother's house. Being that all the lights were off I knew she had to be sleeping, so I just let myself in. Once inside, I went to my mother's room and jumped in bed with her, my mother was in a deep sleep when I got in bed with her, I looked at the time and it was one in the morning I just gave my mother a kiss and went to sleep.

The next morning for a sec it felt like I was back at home with the good morning breakfast smell and all. Even with my dad being gone my mom's always made it felt amazing like when it's a Saturday or Sunday morning and you would wake up and all the kids are running around the house (even though it wasn't like that at all). She was cooking the same breakfast she made the day my dad died. No matter if the house was empty or full she would make cheese grits, eggs, smoked sausage, and cinnamon rolls. It had to be 10:00 in the morning when I got up. My phone was buzzing like crazy and when I checked, it was Blaze.

"You ready?" He asked, sounding alert.

"Um yeah… Let me brush, I'm at my mom's" I said yawning.

It took Blaze twenty-five minutes to get to my mother's. I was waiting out front looking like yesterday when he got out of his car. We greeted one another with a hug, we than got in his car and he pulled off, while driving Blaze told me about what they had done, really I didn't know why the hell was he outside. I looked at him and just shook my head I admired Blaze he was afraid of nothing he moved how he wanted to move nobody told him how to live.

It had to be around six in the morning when we reached Red Bank, New Jersey and stopped at a deli which was closed, there were people walking around doing their morning routine, I looked at Blaze.

"Use your keys," Blaze said.

Once I had opened the door we went straight to the back where we walked up a flight of stairs. There were a couple of apartments up on the floor we got to.

"Open that door." He said pointing to the only black door on the floor. When we walked in there were Statues, Boxes, and Crates, I walked in further and couldn't believe what I was looking at. There were Keys on top of Keys going across the back room wall then there were crates of Champaign and giant cans of protein powder, I was lost by that. I was fucked up by what I was looking at and then he said.

"Everything you see here is a new life for you. My boy wanted to make sure you was good. It's some of the rawest dope over there in those Champaign bottles isn't Champaign at all that's liquid meth which came from his Aunt, that over there in the protein cans don't get confused that's some of the best ecstasy, molly, all types of pills out here. Come on." We went to another room. In the room was four king sized beds and three old fashioned dressers. He said without a smile on his face,

"All this right here is money. It's all yours. You have to become that bitch out here"

I looked around this apartment and couldn't believe what I was seeing, let alone what he was saying. Shit even when he's gone my baby's still was watching out for me.

Now take a walk with me and see how I became a boss.

Chapter 1

Nora

Ever since Blunt died, I took over his empire. But what I done with it was taken it to the next level. Blunt was getting money but he was too local and wanted to stay in Brooklyn. I wanted the whole New York and more. For the past five years, I've been the youngest bitch out here making the kind of money I was getting. I had the streets filled with crack, weed, pills, shit whatever your inside craved, I had, we had the best heroin supplier, mollies, X, we had our own testers, we had everything and everything moved through us, we made sure that our prices as well as our product was the best out. Shit, we even had bars, hookah lounges, and restaurants. Blaze been by my side for the whole ride, schooling me on this life. But he also reminded me that I had a life and not to put all my energy into this. We had cops and judges on payroll so nobody could fuck with us,

It was hot out on the day Melly and I were meeting with this young hustler from out in Cali that's been trying to meet up with me for lord knows how long and I kept blowing him off but something told me to take this meeting.

Melly arranged for us to meet up at a restaurant in Manhattan. We were sitting at the far corner watching everybody as they walked into the busy establishment. Melly was sitting down, sipping on a mimosa yapping about some new dick she was getting, which was getting on my nerves especially now that I wasn't getting any. That's when some guys walked in looking like they were in a rush to be noticed. I looked at the fools and shook my head. I looked at my girl and she said.

"That's him girl." I looked at her in disbelief and said. "You're not serious are you?"

"Look just talk to him. See what he has to offer."

I didn't respond; just let her talk while I watched this guy's movements. I really didn't like what I was seeing. This guy was too loud so I just got up and we all left. On our way out, I didn't know if the mother fucker knew who I was or if he just wanted to be cute, but when the bitch-boy went to touch me, Buck grabbed him by the wrist. His boys jumped up like they wanted to get stupid. I gave the little

Dumb Gotty a looked and asked. "Is all this necessary?"

He looked at the hand that was being dealt to him and all of a sudden got smart when they seen all the guns that was in their faces. They all sat down. Stepping outside, we all had eyes on us. Blaze was waiting by my car with the door open. I looked at my girl but I couldn't be totally mad at her. I just got in my car. Blaze was about to get in but I stopped him.

"No. Go tell Melly to get in here and you drive her car." I put on some music while I waited for her. Once she got in and closed the door, I looked at her and asked, "How long have the two of us been living this life, girl?"

"About four to five years. Why you ask?"

"When have you ever seen me dealing with loud money? Look, you my girl and I'll die for you, but you mess with my money or my freedom then we have a big situation. Let that be the first and last." I looked at her for the first time since she been in the car and asked, "You hungry, girl?"

"Yeah I could use a bite." She responded with a smile.

I drove until we saw a reputable restaurant named Clark Spot. Melly was staring out the window in deep thought.

"You need a dollar?" I asked.

"Excuse me?"

"You look like you need a dollar for your thoughts."

"Shut up, stupid." I just smiled at her comment; that was my girl. She was the only one who would speak to me like that.

I parked my car and we got out. We went inside and there were only a few people in the place, we just sat and waited at our normal seats. I didn't know why but all eyes were on us. Blaze, Mells and Blaze's nephew were at my table while Pop, Missy, and Tree sat at the table beside mine's.

"So what do we have to get done?" I asked.

"I have to head out of town to check on Moe and Tia." Blaze responded.

"Okay, sounds good. Just do me a favor and keep your girls dressed."

"I got it boss. I just hope nobody invites us to a party… other than that, we're good." Blaze said always ready for a war.

After the food came and we had that little family time together (something we do a lot) we all ate, spent a few more minutes in the restaurant, then left.

It's been three days since I've seen my mother, so I drove to see her. I didn't call to let her know that I was on my way. I went to a deli to pick up something to cook. I needed to taste my mother's cooking. I bought her a nice home and hired my mother a nurse. I really didn't want her to be in my pop's house alone.

When I reached my mom's house, a nice red stone in Morningside Heights, I saw her out front talking to her neighbor. I double parked and got out.

"Hey you, old pretty lady!!" I yelled out. Melly got out of the car while my mother and I were in an embrace. "Look at you," I said to my mother, looking at my mother in her green flower summer dress and her green slippers I smiled and hugged my mother.

We all went inside the house and my mother was all smiles. I liked seeing her happy. We were in the den listening to some old-school R&B and I was sitting at the bar rolling a blunt when my mother walked up behind me and said jokingly,

"Yeah girl, light up that dobby." I looked at my mother like she was a spirit.

"What did you just say?" me and Mells asked shocked at what we heard

"I'm just joking. Take that stuff out back."

Mell and I went out back to my mother's patio to smoke and discuss business. My girl was always a little smarter than I was back in school, so I kept her brain on my team. While we talked business, her phone started buzzing. When she picked up and began talking, she sounded afraid. She looked at me like she just heard the worst news.

"We have to go now," she said.

"What's going on?" I asked, worried.

"Moe, his spot just got hit and now he and Kelly is missing."

We got up to leave and I gave my mother some money. After paying her nurse, we left. Once we got back in the car, Melly got on her phone and by the way she was talking, I knew who she was talking to. I looked like I was calm, but deep down I wasn't. I knew which one of the spots got hit. While she was talking on her phone I got on my cell and called Blaze and being that it was her family, she would be the one who have to take care of the situation.

"What you're doing?" I asked.

"I just got the news. I'm on my way," Blaze said.

"No, get a hold of Boe and go to Brooklyn to see what's going on out there, and make sure it stay quiet out there," I said then, hung up.

I really didn't like what was happening but remembering what Blunt and my uncle used to tell me "Never let the loss of a product be the reason of my freedom being lost." I thought just for a sec and told myself that this shit just happens, which it does…to other mother fuckers. Shit like this doesn't happen to me unless somebody sent them.

As I drove, I watched the area and remembered how hungry I used to be when I started working for Blunt. I thought about how grimy and fucked up we were back then I was one of the worst. But in the same hand, I was also the best at what I done. I took Blunts product all over nothing didn't move unless we had a say so. I remember the days and nights with the bullshit hand and hand I had to go home to clean my ass and get out of these dirty clothes.

"I have to get home, girl. Where you want to go?" I asked.

"Just take me to my job."

"No, it's too hot right now. I have to know. Where's my shit? And you…you need to figure out what happened with your people."

After dropping Mell off to her house, I went straight home. I kept Blunts tented glass mini-mansion in Connecticut. I didn't really like the area, it was too quiet, but it was peaceful and that's something I needed. I drove down the marble driveway where one of the help, Elizabeth was working on the flowerbed, my front looked as if it was just mowed I didn't care too much for no guards. I got out of my car and went straight inside where there were three black Donnetti duffle bags on the floor.

"Ma'am this came from your Jamaican partner," another one of the help, Marisol, came out and said. Without looking back at her, I said, "Thank you. I'll take care of it."

I went to my custom-made bathroom. I had my best friend A.B. design and decorate it, and he did his thing… gold frame mirror, white and black ivory and marble ancient tub. He built a glass frame of me on the wall. I ran a nice hot fruit bubble bath. After putting the bags away, I went and got in the tub to think, but the shit I was thinking about…I really didn't need to be.

Chapter 2

Melly

This shit was looking crazy, and if it was anybody else, shit if it was me, I would probably think it. I was pacing back and forth in my office wondering who the fuck was behind that hit.

I sat at my oak wood and sapphire desk, took out my platinum weed chest and rolled up a nice blunt. I lit the tip and took a deep drag and just inhaled. I needed a distraction so I called Noah so he could come over and work me over, but his phone just rang so I just left him a sexage telling him to come over and go to work. I then took out the money book and tried to see how much we lost in that hit. We've never been hit, especially not like that. Now work, money and my family was gone.

What I was trying to put together was since I can remember we have never taken a loss like this, not until these mother fuckers started working for us. I didn't want to think that way especially not with my family but it looked just the way it looked. I took out my cell and was about to call Money but before I could dial the number, Noah called me.

I've been playing games with him for four months. We met while I was making a run; he was in the Bronx selling eighth bags of sour. When I seen him, I liked him automatically. His swag was Ok for a white boy; he wore Burberry from top to bottom. Noah was just moving bud when we met but I had to move his money game up, to a much better product so I got him selling crystal for us and he was making a killing.

I spoke on the phone. "Hello baby," I said, sounding like my pussy was in Miami.

"What you're doing babe?" he asked.

"Busy, just trying to figure this shit out. I was calling you all day. Baby what happened?"

"I know…I was busy. But I do need to see you though."

"Okay. When and where?" I asked.

"Meet me at our spot" he said, sounding a little nervous. I just said "okay" then hung up.

Once I was done with what I was doing in my office I had to go to our old folk's home we uses for money laundering. I went home to shower and change but when I got home, my heart almost jumped out my lovely breast. I saw my life flash before my eyes. In front of my door was five uniformed police. My first thought was to just leave them standing there, but I slowly stepped out of my shiny gold and black Corvette Stingray and slowly walked over to my house.

"Hello, Can I help you with something?" I asked, all perplexed at their arrival.

"Yes you can. Is your name Ms. Baxter?" one of the officers asked.

"Why are you asking?"

"We have a Kelly Monroe in Mount Sinai Hospital. Before going unconscious, she gave us your information. Was that wrong?"

I was standing there listening to what was being said but I didn't want to believe it. My little cousin was unconscious in the hospital and I couldn't do shit. I just slowly walked past them and went inside of my house. I hadn't done what I said I was going to do; I just went straight to the bar and made myself a drink. I rolled me a nice blunt and went to my prayer room asked the big man to forgive me and went on my short journey. I got myself together, smoked half the blunt, and then grabbed my keys. I ran out the house bumping into one of the officers who I thought should've been gone by now.

"What the fuck!!" I yelled at the same time dropping my phone. "What the fuck are you still doing here?!" I asked picking up my now cracked phone.

"We were waiting to assist you" I looked at them like they were crazy.

"No I don't need any help. But I do need you to go find out who the fuck put my cousin in that room."

I jumped in my car leaving them for the second time. I called Nora to inform her on what had happened and where I was going. Once I hung up, I started wondering. Who the fuck could've done that shit to my cousin? I thought maybe that hit was them, and now this? I sped through traffic cutting through cars. Getting to Mount Sinai, I sparked the half blunt that was in the ashtray from earlier. I took that one strong pull, held for a few, than I exhaled.

Reaching this destination was one thing that I really hated doing ever since I lost my child in the one place where she was supposed to have been safe, the hospital. Not even when I was shot, have I stepped in these doors. Now here I am, going to see my baby cousin.

I drove the underground parking lot once I parked my car I quickly jumped out and rushed over to the mechanical doors, I quickly got nauseated at the sight of what I was now seeing, mother fuckers laying on a gurney with either a bullet, stabbed or cop shooting a young black man, I went to the reception desk and as calm as can be I said.

"Hello, excuse me" just to get ignored; this went on about two more times until out of nowhere I heard.

"Bitch don't you hear somebody calling your ass!! Now get the fuck off the phone and do your damn job!" I looked to my side and seen my girl Nora standing there looking like a goddess, she grabbed me close in her arms and gave me a motherly hug.

"Yes. How can I help you?" the dumb ass bitch was so afraid she forgot that I was the one who came for the help.

"You can help me by telling me, where's my little cousin, the police said they brought her here."

"And what's your cousin's name?"

"Kelly Monroe" I said in a painful voice. She begun looking up the name along with the other information I passed her.

"Yes, we do have a Kelly Monroe, she's been placed in the ICU" she said looking at the screen, than she said something Nora or myself wanted to hear "There're police all around her room." after saying that she gave us our passes than she left us continuing her work.

We quickly rushed over to I.C.U. Once we reached the hospital there was like damn near the half of a precinct there. I went to my cousin's room and what I saw, I couldn't believe. I almost fainted at the sight of my baby cousin. Nora and I yelled at the same time, "Oh my god!!" As I looked at Kelly lying there and as I got closer, I saw how bad she looked, breathing tube, eye swollen shut, face beaten beyond recognition and couldn't bear to watch her like that. Nora and I stood over her bed looking at her and a police officer came into the room holding something in his hand.

"Hello Ms. I'm sorry for what happen to. Your?" he stopped not knowing the verity of our relationship.

"Cousin, she's my cousin" I said

"Well my name is officer, Simmons…" Nora stopped him

"Look why are you here? Why aren't you out there? She can't nor can I tell you anything"

"Well that's why I'm here, you see we have some photos of some things that looked out of place so if you can. Can you help us out?"

"I don't see what the fuck that's going to do for you to help but whatever." I said, he stood beside me and showed me some photos from his cell phone and as he passed through I could've sworn I seen something I had custom-made for Noah, so I stopped him.

"Woe, Can you go back a sec?" when he did, it was what I thought.

"Is there something you recognize?" he asked.

"No, it's not" I said looking down, than I said to him, "I'm sorry. Can you please leave us?"

When he left I was stuck for a few seconds. Nora tapped me, getting me out of my thoughts.

"Wake up girl. What the hell is up bitch?" I told her what I'd seen but I really didn't want to think the worst about it. My girl started talking to me but it was like I couldn't hear shit she was saying. I knew that was Noah's chain. But what I didn't know was what the hell was his $3,500.00 chain doing around a crime that my cousin was the victim in?

"Did you hear me?" Nora asked, snapping her fingers in my face.

"What?" I said, returning to reality. "Oh I'm sorry girl. What you say?"

"Look if you feel that it was his, I don't want you to go see him alone. Take Rob with you."

"No, girl, I'm good. Look, I'll hit you up when I'm done."

"You sure, girl?" she asked worried like a big sister. I responded with a smile and a nod.

We sat in my cousin's room for a few more minutes just listening to that damn life support machine. I told Nora I had to go and she said,

"Take this with you just to be safe," and handed me her gun.

"Look, girl, I'll be okay; trust me."

"Love you, mama."

"Love you, sis."

The whole drive home this shit was fucking with my head. I called Noah to let him know that I was on my way. I had to stop home first. I didn't want to think he had anything to do with this situation, but if he did, he's a dead nigga walking. I got home and quickly double parked and rushed inside to get my boy. When I got inside, I rushed over to my safe and got the only black nigga I trust. I changed into my black and white O-looche jogging suit with my black on white Adidas. I took a quick shower and I got dressed and although it was simple I loved how the material hugged my body. My ass looked amazing, and my breasts looked like they wanted to pop out of my shirt. I put my hair in one long braid and finished it off with a white on black O-looche fitted cap. I put my Bugatti in the garage, took out my midnight blue Benz and drove to see Noah.

I drove the forty-five minute drive to the Bronx and went straight to Sound view. It was getting a little dark out by the time I reached my destination. I didn't see Noah's car, so I called. When the line picked up, I heard the same exact sounds that I was hearing around me in the background.

"Where are you?" I asked scanning the area.

"Come in the park, walk to the benches."

I got out of the car and followed his directions. I saw Noah sitting down looking sexy in his grey Donnetti set I bought him three days prior. When he noticed me walking towards, him he stood up, and while I stood there looking at him, I noticed he didn't have on his chain. I didn't need to jump to any conclusions, so I waited. As I looked more when he came closer, I noticed a weird look on his face. I went to give him a hug and his body tensed.

"Hey, baby," I said giving him a kiss. "What's wrong with you?" I asked. He began telling me about what was fucking with him, which was something I hoped he'd never say.

"I'm looking for a partner in our field of work, and before you answer, just know this…your girl is being pushed out of the picture." I stood there allowing him to explain some but then I stopped him.

"Before you finish, let me know something. Where's your chain?"

"I lost it in a spot" he said straight-faced. He then changed his facial expression, "I need you to do me a favor?"

"And what's that?" I asked.

"Know that I will always love you."

After saying that, I felt something sharp going through my back. Then it happened three more times. After that, the last thing I knew was me going down and while falling, the look I seen on Noah's face fucked me up. The nigga had a smile on his face then I was there in total darkness.

Chapter 3

Nora

Damn, leaving that place had me feeling all filthy so I went home to clean my ass. I was about to call Mell but I forgot she was out with that dude. I had to meet up with a new ecstasy and Molly connect I called my boys, Boe and my girl Yani, to come with me. Flow dropped off the duffle bags with the money.

We were supposed to meet up at this dude's lounge, some spot he had in the Bronx somewhere on 243rd street. I really didn't like going out that way for business, but I heard enough about this Red character and now it was the time to put a face to the name. I went through my walk-in closet trying to figure out what I wanted to wear. I had just about every high fashion designer there was. I took out my pink and black O-looche jean faux fur set and my matching sneakers; I gave myself that casual 'hood' look. I kept the hooded jacket open being that it stopped mid stomach I put on a nice O-looche blouse checked me over in my mirror damn I was a sexy bitch, I had the first three button open showing off a little cleavage, I loved the way my clothes hugged my body my jeans gave me that young Serena Williams look, after putting on my sneakers I blew myself an air kiss than reminded myself that I'm that bitch than I left.

On my way out I had my help carry the bags to the limousine, outside Boe was dressed down in a red and white Kenneth Cole two piece with matching hard bottoms he had on a nice white trench coat, he had his new cut shown showing off his curly Mohawk with his pecan complexion, sexy full lips, to speak the truth if he wasn't like a brother to me I probably would give him some. My girl Yani had that comfortable look just like myself, she wore a red and white Fendi short sleeve logo knit dress, on her feet she had on matching Fendi thigh high logo sock boots, she even had on the Fendi red sunglasses, I looked at my girl and just shook my head and smiled.

Boe took the bags from the help than placed them in the trunk after we all got in the car the chauffer got in and once we all was in the inside was so roomy, we had a Navigator limo, once Yani got in we pulled off, I made me a drink from the bar and after fixing my drink I leaned back and just drifted off and started thinking.

We reached 243rd and the area looked like my old area in Brooklyn, (secluded) we drove the little dusty ass one way street I first wanted to say fuck this but I needed this connect, while we drove to the Lounge we took that short right and stopped in front of the Lounge called La Rose the chauffer gotten out to open the door and once we stepped out all eyes touched our movements, Boe was in lead while Yani and myself followed I scanned the area and the people and thought, "But then again I just might make a killing around here.

Stepping inside the Lounge there wasn't anybody in here except the fake bouncer wanna be shooter behind the bar and the real waitress. As we walked fully inside there was a female sitting at the end corner table with a drink in front of her, she looked cute from where I stood, she was dressed in an all white flower print Balmain cocktail dress, her shoes was also fierce, and she was also gorgeous, her deep mahogany complexion, full lips, she also had some enticing bedroom eyes.

I looked around the place and to be the size outside it was cozy and cute on the inside, the waitress came over to us speaking in her Jamaican accent.

"Welcome to the La Rose Lounge please follow me" she said, she took us to the back I guess it was V.I.P "You can wait here I'll bring you a complementary bottle shortly. The boss will be here soon."

We've been sitting in V.I.P for about five minutes until that chic with the flower dress came in accompanied with two of the sexiest well dressed dreads I've ever seen, One was darker then the next, one was tall with long dreads going back in one braid, his skin was so smooth and dark he looked like a God he was dressed in a grey and white suit, white and black hard bottoms, while the other looked like a Jamaican light skinned Shemar Moore, he wore a turtle neck short sleeve black and red Donnetti sweater shirt, black slacks, and some open toe Donnetti man sandals, I looked at her as she walked over, Boe reached for his piece but I stopped him, she looked and said.

"You know it is bad luck to step in someone's home and not speak" I looked at her like she was crazy and said.

"Look sweetie I don't know who you are but I'm not here for any social meeting." the bitch interrupted me.

"Look Nora is it?" I was lost cause I didn't even say my name.

"How the fuck?" she interrupted me again.

"Do I know your name? You see you Americans y'all like to be noticed."

"Look I don't know who the fuck you are and really don't give a shit. I'm here." this bitch was getting on my last nerve with that cutting me off shit.

"You're here to see Red. A person you're coming to do business with, you see Ms. Lee,, yes I know that as well, just like I know that your medical spot just took a big hit and that's why you're here. Am I right?"

"Look the conversation.." I stood up to leave but stopped when I heard her say.

"Ms. Lee, you have a twin whom you haven't seen in years. Your father died when you was a kid" the bitch had my undivided attention "Should I go on? Okay you come here in search of some guy to give you a product. Well you see he won't be coming." I gave Boe and Yani that little smirk but before any movements was made she asked. "So do you have the money?" when she said that I gave her a look like she had God behind her.

"Excuse me?" I asked dumbfounded.

"You came here for business right? Oh where's my manners. Hello love I'm Red." She said extending her hand "Yes you thought I was a guy. Please sit."

We sat back down and waited until the dread came back and when he did he was carrying two grey metal briefcases, while we sat there looking at this bitch I was getting pissed and not at her nor me but at the fact that this bitch was my girl Mells people and she didn't even put me on ahead of time about her movements.

"Would you and your people like anything to drink?"

"No that's okay. We're good." I said staring a hole in her face.

"Yani, Boe, How about you two?" They both shook their heads no at her question. I saw the look in Boe's eyes that he wanted to rest this bitch. So did I, but we needed that connect.

As she opened the briefcases we noticed that it was the product we needed all the pills without a logo on them, I told Boe to make her eyes happy, he opened one of the duffle bags displaying a half a million. Red looked at me and asked.

"Will this be enough?" she asked.

"Yes more than enough. It's been an honor" I said rising from my seat

"You know it's easy for a man to run shit like this and not only him but these people out here would label him a boss, which might be a good thing, but the smarter choice is to put a pretty face like ours… well more of mines to be in the front line"

"Okay I got that. Here you go" I said passing her the money she looked down at the two duffle bags took a stack of hundreds out each bag than said.

"This will be enough. Oh and deer if I would need any more of your time I'll call you. Look my niece is in your care she doesn't know anything of our business and I would like to keep it that way.

Since her father left her mother, and what he done to her after that was unbelievable, but if you don't know of it then it's not meant for you to know. You just make sure my baby girl is good. You got me?" I looked her in the eyes before leaving than I nodded my head towards her than we all left.

We all walked outside carrying two extra cases, along with our money, which was something new to me. The driver was waiting by the car with the door open. We gave him everything except the product. Boe had that with him when, after placing the two duffle bags in the trunk and got back inside, I was thinking about what just went down.

"Call Melly tell her where to meet us" I told Yani.

Blaze bought out a building in Brownsville and that's where we was heading, at this time Yani was still on the phone trying to reach Mells while Boe was sipping on a drink, I was looking out the window and looking at all the stores and restaurants I begun to get hungry.

"I'm starving. What about you?" I asked, they both said yeah, I told the driver where to take us my favorite loft steakhouse restaurant I go to sometime to clear my head. My uncle use to tell me to be a boss you must always move like one.

We've reached Brooklyn at around maybe eleven at night, when we got to our destination I noticed that there was money around from the cars that's been parked outside, once we got out the car my boy Boe looked at me like I was crazy cause the place looked like it was a hot house outside but once we stepped in Yani and Boe both was shocked of the decor but of course as usual I'm underdressed but who gave a fuck this place was like a fancy Mc. Donald's to me.

"Is this my perfect picture Nora!!" the manager said coming towards us looking like she's been in this hot ass place all day, "Come on girl we have your seat right here"

When we took our seat's and I begun to think about the events that took place today and how the fuck did that bitch know all that shit about me and my family? Yani was talking but I really didn't hear shit that she was saying, the waitress came to take our orders, Boe and Yani gave their orders, I told her to bring me a porterhouse steak, baked potatoes, fried asparagus with onion dip and a chocolate mousse.

"Yani call that girl and tell her to bring her ass over here." Once Yani went out to make that call Boe and I talked a little business, it had taken Yani all but three minutes to return I looked at her.

"So?" I asked

"Couldn't get a hold of her, you know your girl how she gets around that Noah dude. She probably got that nigga dick in her mouth right now." I didn't like what she was saying but I just let her speak since she was family, when our food came they brought over a bottle of Champaign we just ate in silence and enjoyed each other's company, once we was done I paid and we left.

We got back in the car and all of a sudden I was getting an awful feeling I looked at the both of my people and asked.

"Which one of you know where that Noah nigga live?" they both said no and as we drove through these memorable street I took out my phone and called my girl but it went straight to voicemail I knew something wasn't right I told the driver it's been a change of plans and told him to drive to Mells house just in case she was on her chick flick bullshit.

On the way to Mells I don't know why but I felt real fucked up inside, I took out my phone and called her again and the shit went straight to voicemail I was getting pissed off and the driver was making me more mad with the speed limit shit.

"Can you speed the fuck up!?" I yelled at him after that he was driving like it matters.

We got to the Bronx and the whole drive I just hopped she was sleeping I couldn't think the way I was, I told the driver to put on some music a Chrisette Michele song came on. When we got to Eastchester my palms begun sweating, we drove to Mells house on Pelham Gardens we stopped at her door and noticed all the lights was off all except the garage, we all got out the car and I took a deep breath and exhaled, we walked to her front door and heard Spanish music playing the door was opened a little like somebody rushed out, Boe opened the door and we pulled out our guns, her placed was a wreck we searched the whole place and everything was gone money, work, and all her jewelry, I was in the room when I heard.

"What the fuck!!" Yani screamed. I rushed to where Yani was when I got to the garage it looked like they just aired it out as I got closer Boe grabbed hold of me and said with a cracked voice.

"No. I don't think you should see her... Not like that boss" while he spoke Yani was looking at the driver's side of the car screaming and crying I broke free of Boe's hold and ran over to where Yani was and when I seen what she was looking at I couldn't believe what they done.

"Oh my god Mells.. WHAT THE FUCK!!!" what they done to her was brutal, her face was beaten in, her throat was cut, she had stab wounds in her face, her thongs was in her mouth not to mention they left her naked and alone, I looked at my team but mainly Boe for times like this. I looked at my girl once more and without turning to face them I said.

"Find his ass and bring him to me. I don't give a damn who the fuck have to die. GO FIND HIM!!" I yelled out I stayed there with my sister holding her in my arms.

Introduction 2

James

I had it rough growing up, yes I get it people have trouble growing up but going from one home to the next not to mention the heinous shit that's been going on while I've been going through those fucking hell places makes a young kid lose it.

My pops died when I was young and at the very moment they placed my dad in the ground my mom's lost it which she was placed in a position where she had to separate us. I missed my peoples but the one I missed the most was my twin, my uncle took her in I didn't get so lucky I went with my oldest cousin and being a kid I been through and seen some fucked up shit. I didn't have that amusement park or Walt Disney life so I made these streets my little playground I couldn't take too much shit living with my cousin so once I turned 11 I ran away but realized later that was just a big fucking mistake, after been placed with a mixed family, the dad would rape the daughter's they had while the moms just let it happen, but she was a devil as well beat on us making the boys feel like shit running from that place going to wherever it was I met Blue on the streets, he was one of the smoothest cruelest teens around the way we clicked right away, I liked his style he had niggaz and bitches on lock he didn't take no type of shit whatever he wanted doe it had better gotten done with no questions asked.

One day he had seen me put some work in on one of the kids around the way. The kid had to have me by three years and a few big pounds but at that moment I didn't give a fuck about shit with all the bullshit I was going though, the guy was getting some hits in but when I knocked him out from that point on my life changed.

Blue and I formed a little clique of the toughest young niggaz and girls from all over the City and we were always hungry, so we had our hands in everything and nobody was safe, the worst of them all was a girl under me name Kiss a mix of Dominican and Jamaican girl she was cute she reminded me of the friend from that old movie called Pretty Woman but with a more up to date look she was bad for a young girl she had that little baby face look going on, her sharp bedroom eyes, she had to be about twelve o thirteen at that time when I seen her. She got the name from one of her hustling uncles it was said that each time she would fight somebody would be walking away with a bloody mouth no matter if it was a guy or girl, she was my girl whenever people see us together we would be called Satan Kiss I would do anything for her same as she would do for me.

My crew and I ran the streets for years, when I turned fourteen Blue got locked up for putting one of the guys who rapped his mother on fire he would've gotten away but came back when they tried to give that charge to me, I knew just as well as he did that couldn't of happen but he wasn't trying to test them and I respected Blue more than everybody that's been in my circle he was the one consistence real nigga so while he was gone I had to be the next up.

Blue was from Harlem so whatever he seen or touched he was able to make money out of, he was smooth and fast with his words and his hustle game and he taught me just about everything he knew.

I was the youngest nigga out in Brooklyn at that time running shit, I even had older guys who knew my brother running shit for us, our bud connect was always on point and we had almost every corner in Crown Heights, we been moving ounces of coke like it was nothing our name was legendary in these streets even as young niggaz a lot of mother fuckers respected us. Blue always told me if you have a good story than you'll have a great audience and if you give a nigga or a bitch just enough then they'll never leave your side I wonder if he was talking about me when he said that.

Everything was going good for me and Kiss until one night I took one of Blue cars out for a joyride with Kiss and two other chic's from the family, I got into a bad accident killing one of the girls injuring the driver in the other car,

Kiss was badly injured but she came out okay, I just had a few scrapes and scars when the cops came I was laid out over the steering wheel but Kiss she halfway out the windshield.

When I came too I was in the hospital handcuffed to the bed when I fully opened my eyes a female officer was sitting in front of the room on her phone. I had to stay in the hospital for three days and when I got out the first place they've taken me to was the precinct, they charged me with Vehicular homicide, car theft and a gun charge and really at that moment I didn't give a fuck.

Living the life I lived I knew this was my future, being in this damn place although at that time I really didn't want to be here but being the type of kid I was I didn't care being in here had me to become the nigga nobody wanted to know.

Now let me tell you how I became hell.

Chapter 4

James

James Penitentiary Flashback

I've been in this place for the last five years and really the only thing that kept me focused while being in this place was the fact that my family will be waiting for me when I got out. Kiss kept me informed on what was going on outside the team was doing what they had to do to continue to eat.

We had a good portion of Brooklyn and the Bronx with us and we done whatever we had to do to make sure we was well known, our hands was in everything the only thing we wasn't doing was that stupid exposing ourselves on the media.

We took over a few areas in the Bronx and Queens I wasn't the one who would bring shit to where I sit. I had to finish this bid I was doing, I had a saying when I walked in here I'm either going to control this or have it to control me, Blue and I kept in touch through Kiss he had fifteen more years to do, I had got news that his moms died which made him lose it, I couldn't wait to get out of here and fast, just the other day there was a young crip kid came in the jail and before he could've even unpack three bloods went in his cell and severely beaten him up when they was done the way his face looked was like he just stepped out the ring with Cain Velasquez which had them to put him in another jail.

Two of my people from outside were in here with me and the same energy we had out there was worse in here. Kiss and I got married when I turned eighteen we had a jail boy being in this place I had to make money so one ofmy boys had the store so if any of these niggaz got hungry they went to my boy Mike, and me and my boy Gee had the drugs, niggaz in here tried us but with no fucking luck, my boys and I had locked the jail down with the blood we had shed when these niggaz come out of pocket, while being in here I wanted to have the same visions I had when I was free but getting comfortable in here wasn't going to happen. One of the female teachers in here was so into me it was like she was my jail wife I had let her give me some sloppy once and every since then I've gotten what I wanted from her, my team and I was the only ones in here with phones in our cells. Ms. Mann, she was one of the best that I've had the chance to experience, the way she done her thing was amazing how she circled her tongue around the head the way her breath felt when she fully engulfed my dick the way she sucked if I was her husband or even her man she would get whatever she wanted and she wouldn't be working here. Ms. Mann wasn't the cutest doll but at these moments of time I just got what I could've gotten from her and if pussy came along then that's what would've happened.

While being in this hell I had to feed my brain so I had to get my G.E.D, I got news that niggaz been trying to take over my spots which has left a few mother in tears, the one thing these dumb ass niggaz need to know is once James own it that's all it is, one night I was in my cell and I called my wife and heard some of the worst news a man in my predicament can hear. She told me that she was picking up some money from my spot with my son when some niggaz ran and shot it up she said that she had gotten hit in her side, but my son and two of my boys wasn't so lucky when I heard that that's when my world has gotten darker.

Two weeks later.

I was sitting in my cell looking at my sons pictures seeing how happy he looked at that moment I felt nothing but hate, I haven't left my cell in a week I was feeling like if I would've left my cell somebody could've lost their life. My boy Gee sent me a text to come out, I really didn't want to but I said fuck it. Although I was in this place my money was still coming hard I threw on my red and white Donnetti short sleeve shirt freshly ironed greens and my red, green and white DN.s after freshening up I just waited for that damn chow alarm, the CO's begun opening the cells, once I heard that metallic click and my cell opened like everyone else was I had stood in front. I've been incarcerated in Elmira for the past two years and I really hadn't had no fun in this place and how I was feeling right now I wanted to go to the circus, before walking out I kissed my sons photo.

Gee, Beast, and myself was walking the yard talking about the situation that happened outside when shit had popped off with some OT Spanish guy came running pass us holding his face which was now leaking with blood, me and my boys was posted on the wall smoking a blunt watching this shit, niggaz was getting stabbed, cut even the chumps was popping off, all this shit went on for about eight minutes until a CO in the watchtower had let off a shot once everybody was on the ground that's when the yard was filled up with the riot squad.

Once we got back inside another fight jumped off between two chumps my boys and I said fuck it and went to our cells, I put on my music listening to a Kendrick Lamar song, I than took out my No Escape book from my boy Mr. Clark and just read a few chapters, I've got hungry so I made a few sandwiches and just let time pass.

Month ½ later

Beast went home and my boy Gee was next, he had three days to go so I told him to stay in his cell. That night I had to go out to make a sell, at first I hadn't felt anything about the scenery; I was out in the yard for maybe forty-five minutes when a Dominican guy came over to me.

"I'm here to get that for Gonzo. He sent me to get whatever it is you have for him." I didn't like the way how this guy was moving so I looked at the kid and said.

"Look I don't know what Gonzo or whatever his name is but I don't know what the fuck you're talking about" as soon as I left I felt something sharp sliding across the right side of my face, at first I didn't think nothing of it but when I spun around I seen this guy they call Y.G standing there and the look he had on his face told me something different I went to touch my face and when I bought my hand back down and I seen my blood that's when I blacked out, I grabbed hold of him and hadn't let go I just started pounding on his face until I seen nothing but red, the CO's started coming towards me but I didn't care I wasn't stopping by the time they got to us he was knocked out with a bloody face they cuffed me than took me to medical.

I was in involuntary protective custody (I.P.C) and couldn't even get Gee any news on what went down, I knew all my shit was about to be found, I was in this cell just thinking Why the fuck did that just happened? I was in the empty cell for about two hours than my cell opened, I looked out and seen my shit at the front it was like they haven't even touched my shit the only shit I was really worrying about was my bed and my sons picture frame when I seen neither was touched I grabbed my things and went back to my cell, once I was locked in I covered the front of my cell took out my phone and sent Gee a message of what happened the officer banged on my cell

"Toilet" I yelled out

"I need to see you Mr. Lee, count time" he shot back growing impatient I peaked my head out allowing him to see me, once I turned back I seen Gee was calling me.

"Yo." I said close to a whisper

"Take it down Mr. Lee" the officer said. Once he was gone I went back to my phone,

"What the fuck happened blood?" I told Gee about what went down he was getting upset but I had to remind him of what's in front of him.

Months later

Once Gee was out I knew it was only a matter of time for me to be next. I had a few days left to get out of here.

The team was still strong even though we lost a lot but we still had the brains. We bought a brownstone in the White plains area in the Bronx, and as soon as Gee got out these doors he went looking for the mother fuckers who took my son from me, he said he got close but lost his connect, I knew what had to be done and really when that gets done I'm going to be sorry for a lot a mother fuckers out there, reflecting on my life my shit was fucked up, my pops died when I was young, my mother losing her mind, my brother died being separated from my twin what the fuck.

I really missed her, I haven't heard from her in years I didn't even know if she was still breathing, shit out of everyone she's the only one that I trust, I heard that, my sister Tricia went off to collage which was good she was always a smart girl even when we was kids she use to always play to be the teacher, damn I miss my people thinking about them I just laid back and drifted off.

Chapter 5

Narrator

While being home James was on a warpath since he walked out of Elmira prison doors, he's been searching for the person or people who killed his son, and from the way he's been moving there was nobody safe, whoever had a name became his victim and there was nobody who could calm him down.

James was in his bedroom with his wife when his cell went off, he checked it and seen that it was his boy Bang, James just wanted to spend a little time with his wife but he still answered.

"Bro I'm with my wife. This shit better be important"

"Yo get over her on 196 and Valentine, and hurry up" Bang said out of breath.

"What the fuck is up?" James asked while hopping out of bed he quickly gotten dressed, he grabbed his wife keys to her midnight blue Lexus, before leaving he moved the portrait of his family opening the safe and took out his black Glock 19 and beside it was his wife's nickel platted edition, after securing his safe he quickly left the house once he got in the car he didn't wait another second for the tires to screeching the pavement.

At this moment James didn't really care about whatever he was walking into' but he did know Bang and how his brain worked (always on pop off) so he had a feeling that he had to do some work.

The two had a strange bond, they met while both families was going to war and at one of these wars one of James top people was cornered by the police on Bruckner blvd and bang and one of his boys came and shot all their way out, when James got news while being in his cell every since then James been coming through for bang and vice versa.

Driving down 196 James noticed Bang standing around Latin hustlers was standing around and there was also another Spanish guy sitting on the ground looking like he just came out 3rd round with Roy Jones JR James quickly doubled park and hopped out of his car, he looked at his boy than the bloody face surrounded by the hounds he walked over to the crowd then knelt down and asked.

"Why have this happened to you?" he asked

"I..I..I don't know" he said afraid of the outcome whatever it was. "Your boy asked me a question about somebody than he just started beating my ass."

"So who was he asking about?" James asked already knowing the answer.

"That's just it I don't know who he was talking about. Some guy that killed some kid" he asked with tears forming in his eyes.

"Well I'm going to ask you and I'll be doing that only once, now the choice is yours to walk or have 6 men carrying you " as James spoke to him he looked at the hand he just been dealt. "Now from what I can remember I had a son but today I don't have that son. Do you know why is that?" he looked deep into James stare, the boys heart was beating rapidly and although the weather was cool he was drenched in sweat James looked at the guy as he took out a stick of double mint gum passing the guy one.

"What your name is kid?" James asked

"What..Why?" he said with tears perplexed by the question.

"It's only right to know whom I am sharing my words with. I'm sure you know who I am"

"My names R. jay"

"Okay R, look I'm sure you want to see how beautiful tomorrow is going to be? So please R be smart" James said displaying his boy he looked down at what James was now showing him and R. Jay said fuck it.

"I don't know the dude..I knew his girl, I overheard her telling her friends about what her man done I swear I don't know who done it"

"Okay so where can we find his bitch?" James asked.

"Why? She haven't done anything"

"Look, who's the one with the gun? Right now all I need you to do is let me know what I need to know"

Once James got the information that was needed he looked hard at R. Jay placed his arms over his shoulders and said with a stern stare.

"One thing a man should never do is fold under pressure and I see that's something you do often so here's what's going to happen, you see these young men right here is going to take you to that building over there but you see the only thing is you won't be coming back"

James, Bang, and a few of the block goons all went looking for this chic Fendi from Brooklyn James was in lead he knew if she wouldn't let him know what he needed to know than he knew without a doubt she'll be a dead bitch but no matter what the situation is James never raise a hand to hit a woman but he had someone who loves too. He called his wife and told her about what's going on and that he was coming to get her, after he hung up he called Bang.

"Yo" Bang answered putting the finishing touches on his nicely rolled blunt.

"We're going to pick up my wife" he hung up his cell and put on some music.

Approaching his home he noticed his wife standing there looking like she was ready for war, she had on an O-Looche fatigue set with some forest green and black Nikes, she had her hair done in one single braid covered by an O-Looche head wrap her face looked like she was Vaseline up. James smiled at how his wife was always ready for anything. James stopped and got out after given one another a hug and kiss they got in the car and pulled off.

Chapter 6

Kiss

I was resting when I heard my cell, I got up still groggy but I had to stop this annoying sound.

"Hello" I said still sleeping.

"Babe I'm coming to get you" the sound in his voice was telling me something was wrong and as he spoke I couldn't believe what I was hearing I quickly hung up took a quick pussy clean and then got dress I put on my O-Looche thong set with my O-Looche black and green fatigues, I put my hair in a braid put on a matching head wrap, I threw on some Vaseline couldn't afford any scratches on this gorgeous face I gave myself that last look over and started leaving, my gorgeous green fuck me eyes my flawless caramel complexion plump juicy lips all a bitch could say was damn I'm the shit, I went to get my best toy when I opened the safe I noticed he had taken his after hoisting my gun I went out to wait for my man.

Every since the day it happened we was on a manhunt looking for even just one of the motherfucker's, now my baby said that he had some information. I've been waiting for maybe like five or ten minutes until I seen his car pulling up he also had a few cars behind his, I casually walked over to him and like a man he got out gave me a husband's embrace once we got back in the car we pulled off, my daddy was focused while he drove, although he's been in prison for the last 5 ½ years this was our son and there's nothing I can say to stop him, not that I would.

When we got to Brooklyn the first area we went to was East New York, I didn't know who we was looking for or how the bitch even looked, not even a name for that matter, James had a phone that I never seen he passed it to me than said.

"That's who we're looking for" he said pointing at some pretty looking chic "Her man is the one responsible for our son being dead" as I looked at the bitch it was like this was the only doll I ever wanted to play with.

We been around East New York looking for this bitch, when we came up empty we went to terrorize Bed Stuy once again nothing. I could tell my baby was piss but he wasn't trying to let it be shown and as soon as we was about to give up I noticed one of the other bitches that was in the photo with her, she was standing in front of a Bodega with some dude I yelled to my baby.

"Stop the car!!"

"What the fuck babe?" he said stomping on the breaks.

"Look" I said gesturing to the bitch when he seen who I was talking about he put on a Damien devilish smile, I got out and when I did that's when Bang and everybody else has gotten out, motherfucker's was so into their own situation mother fuckers wasn't even paying attention (Brooklyn shit) nobody beef nobody care.

We all approached the bitch, I looked at the guy who was with her and asked.

"Is this your girl?"

"Nah I just met her. Why?" he asked looking around at everybody.

"Look at whose asking" I said gesturing to everybody he just took her phone and I guess deleted his number cause once he gave it back he jumped in his car and pulled off once he was gone I looked at her and said.

"As you seen from your boyfriend today is the time to make smart choices." I said putting my arm around her shoulder "Look we have to go chat"

"Look whatever is going on I don't got shit to do with it I don't know your man or I doubt.." I laughed at the bitch and said.

"This bitch think this is about some dick" we all started laughing "Get your ass in the car, while we done our work people was cellcording but at that moment none of us gave a fuck, we was now in the car going back to the Bronx and then I thought about a much better spot in Manhattan while sitting in the back seat with the bitch I said to my baby.

"Go to Manhattan over there by 207 Bridge."

"What's over there?" he asked not looking back at us

"Trust me babe go over there it's the best place to go where I can have fun with my doll" I was saying this while playing in her hair with my gun, she was close to a cry attack telling me about her son and all that bullshit family bullshit "Okay since we're talking about kids and family seems like we're going to have a fast and understandable conversation right?"

We've reached 205 which was a dead end area, we got to the area where we was going and when I looked at the bitch she seen that this was more than business, it was getting a little dark, the grocery store was now shutting down which made the situation better for me, as soon as the car came to a stop that's when she begun hyperventilating once she seen the East River.

"Get out" I said now with my gun aimed at her.

"Ok,, ok,, ok I'll stop whoever he is I'll stop seeing him" I couldn't take the begging so I got out dragging the bitch by the hair, there was a little sitting area overlooking the East River. Once James and I got in the little park we had Bang and his boy block both exits' I took out some bud and rolled up a blunt and James and I placed our guns along with the phone on top of the stone checker board table.

"Please sit down" James finally spoke, I just lit the blunt.

"Look you think you're being here is because of some dick? Sorry love it's not" I showed the girls Fendi picture along with her and some other bitch. "You being here is about this bitch right here" I said to her now with a death look in my eyes and the only thing that would keep her away from it would be her respond. "Who is she?"

"That's my sister Roxy. Why you ask?"

"So this should be easy with no lies right?" when I asked that question she stood up and reached for one of the guns but my man's reflex was quick.

"Please sit down and don't have me to speak again or my next words will be telling them to kill you, Now be smart and talk to her or swim in this river without moving your damn arms." James said aiming his gun in her face.

Once she sat back down and begun being rational I started getting all the information I needed about this Roxy or Fendi bitch. My husband and I got up and took our things than we left leaving her behind when we left the area we got back in our car while we waited Bang came over to the car and asked.

"What you want to happen with her?"

"Have you and your boys ever played with a doll?" I asked

"Hell no! What the fuck do we look like?"

"Good unlike other girls they worry about how boys treat their toys well Bang I don't. You and your boys could do what you like with my doll. Do what you want have some fun."

I called the number that she gave me, I called private it rung a few before she picked up sounding like she was fucking.

"He-elloo- agghh" I just hung up looked at my man and smiled.

We haven't went to her right away we allowed her one more night of fun, we was on our way home than I thought about it, my son died in my arms and my husband didn't have the chance to get to know his child he even stopped trying to have another one, I gently rubbed his knee he looked at me I smiled and said.

"Go get the bitch" I said than we were on our way to Marcy project.

Chapter 7

Narrator

They left her bloody beaten body in the sitting area in the cold night, she's been beaten, stabbed, cuts all over her brutally bloody body, and her face was broken in many places. What they've done to her was gruesome how they left her was nasty not even a dog deserves this gruesome act.

The weather was cold out when three young Spanish hustlers that lived in one of the buildings in Dyckman projects came walking in along with two teen girls they had tagging along to the area to smoke some hookah and some bud when one of the girl seen the stiff body that's been left almost naked she yelled out and ran shocked of what they seen the teens not never being this close up to a dead body before calling the cops they all took out their phones and begun taking photos of them with the body. (Most likely to put on the gram)

Bang was only a few blocks away on University puffing on his freshly rolled blunt waiting for a phone call from James, while he sat in his ivory white Benz watching his money being made he was enjoying all that was going on at the moment.

Bang was at least one of the deadliest nigga in the Bronx shit in New York period, every since he lost his brother he lost all care for human life, Bang cell had went off he looked at the number and smiled as he answered.

"Yo Bang meet Kiss and me at Marcy projects, Now" James said.

"Bet" was all that's been said while checking his gun stopping the beautiful Spanish female that was now engulfing his manhood "Okay go home" Once the girl was out of his car he revved up his engine and pulled off, while driving to Brooklyn heading to Marcy he seen a mob of police cars and ambulance was zooming pass knowing where they were going Bang smiled at the thought of what's going to be found when they get there,

They wanted anybody whose close to the bitch know that they're on the way, Bang was relentless and so was his followers and James got close to him for that one reason, but just the same as James was smart so was Bang.

While Bang was driving down the Concourse his phone started buzzing he pressed his Bluetooth earpiece.

"Speak" was his only response and as soon as he heard her voice he knew it was a blood bath needed to be done, when a deal went bad with one of her dealers and when Bang took care of it she knew she could always call on him, but most of all she could trust him.

"Bang I need you it's about your sister hurry she's she' gone Bang. Mells she's..she's dead" out of everything Bang had ready for his day this wasn't one of them, now this was the one reason to pick up his gun Bang quickly came to a sharp stop on Grand Concourse almost causing his own demise with the City bus when he heard what was said,

"Who done it too her?"

"We have a thought but we can't find the dude "

Bang hung up the phone and pulled off on his way to Brooklyn he decided to call James.

"Yo what's good Bee" Kiss responded

"Yo sis where's my boy.

James and Kiss was sitting out front of Marcy projects waiting in their car watching their targets building' they've been sitting in that spot for the last hour and a half, both Kiss and James was well known throughout of Brooklyn and just like when Jay Z links with Beyonce it's going to be something big and people knows when they see the two of them together they know somebody is going to be added to the final breath list.

There were a bunch of unfamiliar cars was around the area and nobody wanted to nosey, Kiss called the number of the girl she was looking for.

She was upstairs in the kitchen fixing breakfast for her and the new guy that's been in her bed, Roxy was a gorgeous chic but her choices of men was never good, she had her mother's lovely copper complexion, along with her shiny long black natural hair, her body was a few notches under that female rapper from Queens but only difference was Roxy was all real, her smoke grey eyes, inherited from her pops Roxy was on her way back to her man when her phone begun ringing when she seen the number she smiled ready to brag about her night but when she picked up all she heard was deep breathing after hanging up standing in front of her room Roxy was now focused on her morning friend that was now facing up in the air, she licked her sensuous lips and savagely went for him.

In the stairway there were four of James guys going up while James, Kiss, and three of the girls that came took the elevator to the 7th floor and knocked on the door, Fendi was so focused on her company she just opened the door for death, thinking that it was her friend and as soon as the door was opened the only thing Roxy seen in her face was guns, James placed his fingers over his lips motioning for her to back up, once inside her friend came out the room still naked with his manhood sticking straight out, once his attention was on the company he tried running back to the room but stopped once he heard that frightening sound, the two has gotten bound and tied to a chair, One of the guys that came they calls Gunz took off a black bag and placed it on the table when he opened the bag and placed it contents on top the table Fendi begun pissing on herself.

"Whoa,, whoa. What's happening? What the fuck.." Kiss covered her mouth pulled a seat in front of her and sat down, took out her cell phone and had a photo of her son and said.

"We are here for one reason and one reason only and the only person who can help us and yourself is you Ms. Fendi." She said pointing in her direction. "You see.." James stopped Kiss by cocking his gun getting Fendi's full attention.

"I'm not as gentle and kind as my wife. My son is dead and your man done the deed he killed my son shot my wife and robbed my spot three strikes. I want him dead"

"Now what I'm going to do is take this off your mouth and you're going to help us. Am I right?" Fendi looked at Kiss than at the table where she seen that there was a blowtorch, knives, a sledgehammer and some drug needles with her eyes forming teary she nodded her head yes "Okay Black" once her mouth was uncovered she silently said a prayer she looked for her male friend and seen that they worked him over he looked severely beaten.

"I'm going to ask you once. Where'd your lil man go?"

"My lil man?" she asked confused by the question she said "What the fuck are you talking about?" she asked frighten.

"Yes your lil man that done that robbery. You know the one you were bragging about to those other bitches you hang out with. I want you to look at him, just know he's innocent through this shit, he haven't done nothing wrong in my eyes, but you on the other hand. Well you're in some shit"

Roxy looked while Kiss gently rubbed the blowtorch her heart begun to beat rapid, Kiss gave Guns a nod and he untied one of her hands and placed it on top of the table, Kiss picked up the sledgehammer sat back down and gave Fendi a look.

"Well?" Kiss asked

"I don't know.."

"Wrong answer" Kiss said smashing Fendi's pinky with the hammer, yelling in pain Karina one of Kiss number one hitters covered her mouth than Kiss asked.

"Where is he?"

"Look I swear I don't.."

"Wrong again" Kiss said smashing another one of Fendi's finger. "I can go on all day; I just need you to know you have but so little fingers left. Look think about you don't be one of those dumb bitches that has to die for some small dick"

"Sonny never tells where he goes, he just come and go I swear I don't know where he went"

"Okay let's say that we believe you. When will he be coming back?"

"Two days from now I can call him. Please I don't want to die" she begged for her life.

"Give me the number. Matter of fact I want his whole damn phone and address info. His mother, dog, kids I don't give a fuck I want them all." once she has gotten the information needed, Kiss smiled stood up bent down to face her and said.

"What's going to happen to you, I want you to know is cause of the choices of dicks you choose to suck this isn't because of what your man done. So, Fendi's your name huh? A hot brand right so with that being said I want you to go out in a blaze." After saying this everybody exited the apartment all but James and Kiss. James douched Roxy with alcohol while Kiss flamed up the blowtorch as Roxy watched the flame she tried begging and pleading, James turned up the music after pouring alcohol over her body they both stood there as Kiss placed the bitch on fire they both stood there watching as her body start to crackle and her flesh turn from pink to purple to black to burn same as her male friend, she made her last scream, before leaving the apartment while Roxy and her man bodies burned James and Kiss took the back exit not trying to be seen.

Once outside all the cars that accompanied James and Kiss was nowhere to be seen the couple got in their car and pulled off, there was a cloud of smoke along with a big blaze of fire was forming out the building James looked at his wife and asked

"What now?"

"Continue getting this money, this situation will get handled. Go home I need to change and clean my pussy"

"That's my pussy" James responded with a smile while the two drove off.

Chapter 8

Nora

Bang myself and a couple of my people were out here terrorizing the Bronx looking for this Noah mother fucker, when we couldn't find him we called it a rest, I placed eyes on every situation that had some money coming in looking for this asshole Bang was standing in his own world when I said to him.

"Bee is you okay? We're going to get him I promise"

"Yeah I know. I have to call my boy"

"Okay. By the way I hear a lot of this guy. What's his name? What does he do?"

"It's my boy Jay. His son got killed in a robbery; I have to check him out"

"Not a problem, just get back with us". I said than I went to my car, when I pulled off I wanted to go home but I had money that needed my attention.

I reached my office, I liked coming here a spot I made happen with my brain and my blood and a lot of my sweat I sat at my white mahogany wood desk, and looked over our numbers which looked great I had to get to my business that took care of all our money laundering, while leaving I glimpsed at a picture I had of my twin and I when we was around maybe three or four, I missed him more than anything, I haven't seen or heard nothing of him since we had to separate, I just hope wherever he's at he's good.

I had to do a money check Blaze was on his way back from handling our business in Colombia, I don't think Blunt dealt with them when he was here that's why he never done business with them, but me I want my money coming from every angle and I really like that money I couldn't trust, just in case they was to try me that gives me all the reason to open the doors to a few churches, I had to call Belinda she was over all the money that came through Heaven Awaits doors which was a home for old citizens I opened it just for that one reason we also own, a pool hall a couple of clubs and two hookah lounges and a restaurant, the boys was on my lace front for a while that shit made me get a nice job to keep them off my ass.

Blunt told me if I can't enjoy the thrill don't go in the park, and me I can't get enough of the fun.

I got in my car and was on this money run, I needed to go on this money run I needed them to see the face of the bitch that's coming to them if my empire was to collapse.

Getting here was fast when I reached I noticed some of the residents walking around acting like this was their last home as soon as I walked through the mechanical doors my phone started buzzing.

"Yes" I answered nonchalantly

"It's Belinda"

"I'm in the lobby, and step on it"

Belinda came down holding a steaming cup and a pad. Belinda was my old boss niece and although her aunt was a bitch she and I just clicked she was one of my best looking girls, her hair was done up in a short curl cut wig (which she don't need) but it did allow her puffy cheeks to be shown she had the cutest nose, her brown eyes looked like it told a powerful story, her luscious pouty lips that looked so succulent, she was thick but she knew how to make all her curves work for her, she had on a cream and black O-Looche snake print dress which looked great on her.

"Your caramel macchiato" she said giving me the hot cup.

"Keep it I just want to see my money"

We took the elevator to the bottom floor and we went to my safe, when the safe got opened my eyes brightened at the sight of what I seen, I took out my book to check all my money comings, I told Belinda to leave and went over them alone, once I was done I took out my two money counting machine I called her back in to help me count this money.

"Yes. You called?"

"Yeah get this machine and help me with this, and when we're done I need you"

As soon as we begun counting my phone started ringing I didn't recognize the number so I answered.

"Lee. Who is this?"

"Hello this is Nurse Benson we're calling to inform you that we have a Margret Lee she says she's your mother" when I heard what was being said I stopped everything.

"What Hospital?" I asked

"Montefiore"

I quickly rushed out leaving Belinda to finish up. As soon as I got out I called Blaze but he was still in the air, I called Bang I was rushing pass these damn New York drivers.

"Where's the situation?"

"It's me, I'm the situation"

"Whoa, whoa, whoa baby girl was sup?" he asked sounding worried

"It's my mom she's in the Hospital"

"Which one I'll be there; but I'm with my boy"

"Bring him I'll be at Montiforie"

When I reached the Hospital I couldn't believe it Bang's car was already there, I rushed in and seen the help she came running to me with tears.

"Ms. Lee" I had to stop her.

"Look I don't want to hear any of that just let me know where my mother is" I said. After Bang's boy and I introduced ourselves we went to sign in we got our passes and went to my mother's room, when we got there she was laying down looking at the ceiling, when I walked in and seen my mother in that bed my heart begun speeding up, the Doctor came over to me looking real delicious.

"Hello my name is Dr. Lawrence I'm here to let you know that your moms will be okay, she had a mild heart attack, and we're going to keep her for observations."

I went and stood next to my mother and begun wondering what would happen if my mom's wasn't here, first my pops than my brother my man, best friend, what the fuck was going on. My mother looked at me and smile.

"You scared me young lady" I said lightly tapping her on the shoulder

"I'm so glad to see the two of you together, God bought you home to me" she said at first we thought she was talking gibberish

"Ma what are you talking about? I'm always going to be here" she looked to face Bang friend and said.

"Not you girl, Why are you over there boy?" Bang started walking over to my mother but she stopped him and said. "No not you Brian I'm talking to my son" I looked at my mother like she was losing it.

"Ma what the hell are you talking about?"

"I don't believe it you two are right here in the same room and you're acting like stranger's" when she those words I was lost I looked back at who was still here and only two guys in the room I already knew one"

"Ma what are you saying?" the girl asked.

"I'm saying that's your big head brother standing over there. James bring your butt over here"

Chapter 9

James

We all was confused at what was being said especially me being that my name was being called out; I stepped out of the shadows of the room and slowly walked towards the center. I know I've been separated from my family when I was young and haven't heard from any of them in years but this shit here was crazy.

"Excuse me ma'am" I said nervously

"I'm sorry I was.." the girl they call Nora stopped her

"Ma are you saying that he's.."

"Yes that gorgeous man standing there is your twin" she said to her than she looked my way than fucked me up "James Prince Lee born in Brookdale Hospital November 7th should I keep going boy"

I didn't understand what was going on I didn't know what I should've done so I guess my twin took care of it when she came over to me and gave me a big hug, I had backed up to take a look at her, for years I haven't seen or heard from either of them and here they are, my phone started ringing at first I was going to just let it ring but hadn't so I stepped out the room for a sec.

"Talk to me"

"Babe where are you?" Kiss asked

"If I tell you, you wouldn't believe it; but let me deal with this and I'll hit you back when I'm done" I said to here than went back in the room

A doctor was now in the room looking over her, Bang, Nora, and I went out to go catch up she told the nurse help to go to the room than we left the Hospital.

When we got outside while we walked Nora was looking like we was her bodyguards, I was still a little messed up about the news but I kept my cool.

"So twin" she said "What's… hold on the kid that Bang told me about. Was that your kid?" we walked and talked I told her about my target and she told me about hers, at first I didn't know what to say cause I didn't know the girl not even through Bang and that was his sister.

"I know what we should do" Nora said

"What's that?" Bang retorted

I couldn't keep standing around like shit was all good especially not when I had money to make and a nigga to kill out here in these streets.

"Look no offense to your mom's brain or her vision but I have shit to take care of and a bitch to kill" I said leaving the restaurant

"Look don't go" Nora said grabbing hold of my arm "It sound crazy to me as well but what if it's not what if you're my twin?" she asked, I looked at her and put on a devilish grin.

"Then I feel sorry for this City"

"This would tell you if you're my twin"

She reminded me of a picture we took together she also reminded me of the day the cops had came to my mother's house, when she said that I knew I was talking to my twin, I cleared my eyes and asked.

"So twin Who gets it first?"

"That's going to be big, but first. Where's this wife of yours?"

The three of us sat in the dinner and reminisced while eating one of our favorite meals lasagna, we sat for a little while longer than she said something I haven't heard in years.

"We need to get back to mom"

We got back to hospital when we got back to my mother's room where she was giving everybody a hard time she said to Nora

"I want to go home"

"Ma chill you" than she looked at me "It would be nice if you help"

"Okay" I said

I kindly walked over to put her clothes on with her slippers and we walked out.

"What the hell are you doing?" Nora asked

"Look she's grown the doctor said that she was good she want to go home so let's go"

Once we were outside I called my wife on face time.

"Hey babe where are you?"

"I'm with Bang; but I have.." before I could say anything Nora snatched my phone.

"Hey sis" she said to my wife

"Who the fuck was that?" my wife asked about Nora

"Babe I'm coming home now. I need you to meet somebody real special to me."

"Is they more important than me?"

"Please don't ask me that?" I said with smile.

We got to my house I noticed my wife's car, I parked beside her car than got out, Bang followed once I helped my mother out the car, we all went inside my house once inside I called out to my wife when she came out she looked radiant we all went to the living room.

"Everybody except for Bang, this here is my queen" while I was talking Kiss phone started ringing when she went to answer we left my mother and her nurse while the kids went to talk business, we went to my studies

"So you're doing this good huh?" Nora asked

"This is okay but I don't want to talk about my placed we need to figure this out"

"I'm thinking about something but after that we need to talk about business."

"Look I got shit going on out here; I'm not trying to disturb right now all I want is a bitch dead"

She told me about what she was thinking about doing which was a smart plan and really it was smarter than mines,

Kiss came in with a bottle of Champaign and some already rolled blunts.

We stayed in my studies going over what was supposed to be done, we left my studies to an aroma I haven't smelled in years, my mother was in the kitchen cooking, being that time wasn't on the light side they all stayed over. We stayed up having fun going over the plans.

"So boy what do you got going on out here?" Nora asked

"A little bit of everything."

"And how strong and reliable are your team?"

"You'll see soon enough" was all I said.

Chapter 10

Nora

With the time we been spending together nobody was safe, I took some of my twins team and he done the same with mine. Nobody was able to make shit while we were looking for these two bitch niggaz. James went to the west coast, Kiss stayed back to run their business, there was a call saying one of our targets was seen going in a rite aid on Fordham being that was Bangs area I told him to take care of it,

"Yo Nora. Where is it?" Bang said

"Where are you?"

"Around the way looking at this money get made. What's up?"

"Good go to Rite aid that nigga mother just walked in there, go get that bitch and bring her ass to me and I want her to be breathing." I said with a stern tone

I had to go check on my mother since James and I bought her a house and got he some more home care, I didn't know why but she wanted to go back to our old home being that we couldn't we bought my grandmother's home, I wished thing's could've been much better for her but at least twin and myself can make things a little better, I got in my car put on my girl Mary J Blige and listened some real music, I thought about the shit that I got for this City but the best shit I have for this city is my twin my best partner, now we can make Scorpion Sting the way it really suppose to be and with my connects along with his and his muscle out here we'll make an Empire that man Lucious and Cookie could've learned from twin had the green and white along with two stores one was a clothes store and the other was a liquor store in his mind if him or his people don't get money than nobody else can. I also liked his wife she seemed to me she's a rider like she was there for him from the start, and even when they son died she stayed by his side, I could see the pain and I know that she won't be happy until this Sonny nigga just see night.

I got to Brooklyn and hurried to Crown Heights when I drove down my old block the shit looked real different from the last time I've been here, damn I remember I didn't have shit not even a bike now I'm driving down these streets in an all white and grey new edition Kit I seen my mother sitting out front with the help, I felt like royalty when I stepped out my car my phone started buzzing.

"Yeah"

"What's this shit I'm hearing about you?" my uncle asked, my uncle and I haven't spoken for years since he found out what I do

"What you talking about?"

"Look I got a call from up top" I had to stop him.

"Unc I'm visiting my mother I don't have the time for this"

"I'm on my way"

After we hung up I went to my mother, I still don't know why she came back out here, I noticed an old friend of mine still out here same house same thot attitude with two rug rats.

"Hey Nora was sup girl"

Hey Shianne," I said to her looking at her with disgust.

"Damn girl you looking real great" she said

"Thanks girl, and you… you well looks the same" I didn't want to stand here having a long tedious conversation if it wasn't about money, in a sad way I feel bad for her, I left her standing alone with her two kids when I got to my mother she was laughing with the neighbor.

"Hey young lady"

"Look at my baby" my mother said smiling "Where's your twin?"

"Taking care of business ma"

We went when my uncle pulled up when he stepped out his all black Rolls Royce jeep, when he looked at me I felt like that bad little niece that was about to get her ass whoop. Every since my dad died my uncle stepped up and raised me as his own daughter and at times maybe a little better, I didn't believe what he was playing, when he stepped out of his car my uncle looked like he belong on a poster he was wearing a Donnetti grey and white three piece suit with the matching hard bottoms looking like a light skinned Steve Harvey, I love my uncle but right now with the look in his eyes I didn't know what to expect.

We got in the house my uncle and I went to the sitting room to talk.

"So little girl, let me know what's going on with you?"

"Some nigga named Noah had…" he cut me off

"Look I know you're not about to say one of your people went to sleep"

My uncle and I spoke for a while and everything he said was the truth this is a life we all live, jail, and death is a real part of this life. When my uncle was in his money days he had the whole Brooklyn on lock, he was the shit but he backed away from that life when his wife died in his arms from a shot that was meant for him, I like talking to my uncle Derek but this conversation I wasn't with, so I said.

"Uncle Dee, I know you're not trying to stop me from doing this especially after what happened to your son and.." I had to stop him from his next words.

"Don't.. look there's ways to do things, I'm getting calls about my niece is out here doing dumb shit" he stood up and came to me "Look there's way's to take care of this and the way you're moving I taught you better than that."

I told my uncle that my twin was back he just looked at me and shook his head like he was saying "Oh my god" my mother walked in that gave me enough room to leave, my uncle told me to slow down I just laughed because it was no slowing down now and reminded him

"Unc this city was renamed to Nor York tell your top men to stop calling" I called Blaze when I walked out the little dirty kids on the block was all around my car with their filthy hands on my shit, I got in my car but before I drove off I gave them all twenty dollars than I pulled off. I didn't understand why the fuck was my uncle being called it's not like I worked for anybody. I'm my own boss and it's not like he can stop anything from happening, my cell went off.

"Yeah" I said

"What you want done with this old bitch?" Bang asked

"I'm coming now just hold her right there"

I called Kiss and told her where to meet me, I had to go to my house to pick up my bitch I just hopped when Kiss see her I hope she'll be smart, when I got home I seen 3 cars in my driveway I didn't know who so I called my boy Boe.

"Boss"

"Come over to my place" I said to him than hung up.

I was never one of those bitches that like to bring unnamed attention so security was never needed. I sat in the my car watching these dumb motherfucker's for like ten minutes when I seen Boe's car pulling up I also seen two of my other people walking down looking like normal pedestrians, he hadn't even reached half way down the block until I stepped out of my car, Boe got out of his car and the first thing I noticed is that he didn't come to talk, I looked at his chrome 357 Beretta, no matter how much I love his bravery sometimes I think his movements are careless, nevertheless I make sure to keep him close.

"Put that away" I said to him, side by side we approached the driver's side of one of the cars, when the middle car opened some young Rick Ross motherfucker stepped out walking up to me with his hands extended, he said.

"Pardon my intrusions but.." I stopped him from talking

"Who the hell are you? And why the hell are you on my property?"

"Look my reasons for coming is not to alarm you I just needed to put a face to the reason of my low income that's going on" than he looked around "This is a lovely set up. Hum no security, you know you're real cute little girl, Go back to school and stop playing these games"

Before the dumb mother fucker could've gotten back in his car I said.

"Whoa, whoa, whoa, you come on my property and think you could play top nigga and walk away? Um no you're fucked" I walked away and let my team sort out the problem for me. It be times like this that I always have the highest respect for him he don't talk or ask questions he just go to work, and so did those who I placed behind him. Boe and his people took no time in going to work by putting an ass whooping on every last motherfucker that wasn't invited on my property when they got done that's when thing's had started getting more interesting. Boe and his boys didn't give a damn about who would've been watching they've open their trunks to each of their cars throwing motherfuckers in and then pulled off.

Chapter 11

James

It was hot out here, meeting up with this connect that twin needed me so desperately to meet, I bought a few of my best hitters she had that Blaze cat come with me.

When we got off the plane there were three Benzes waiting for our arrival. I gave Blaze a look when one of the doors opened.

"Just chill, we good"

I didn't know why was I'm here the only two things important to me was to finish these two niggaz off and continue getting money all this in between shit was crazy to me.

Twin was telling me about her business and what she needed me for, at first I thought it was stupid but when I thought about it, it's really a smart one, Blaze was talking to the dudes when something caught my attention some kid was taking our pictures, I casually walked over to him and said.

"Can I see your phone please?" the kid was no more than 10 but he looked like he was up to something, when he gave me the phone I seen at least seven pics of us, Blaze came over

"Leave the lil nigga alone and come on"

"Look at this' I said passing him the phone when he seen what it was he gave the kid some money than took the phone.

"That simple now let's go"

While driving to wherever we was going my hand was planted on my gun, even though Blaze was showing that we was still good I didn't know these niggaz and where I'm from new hood new problems and right now I didn't need no new situations on my plate.

Blaze and the dude who was driving passing a blunt to each other they wanted me to hit but I passed needed to stay on point. We had to be driving for like maybe forty-five minutes when we pulled up to a nice looking powder blue stucco; Blaze looked back at me and said.

"We're here bro. Yo you need to listen to everything that's being told to you. Nora needs you to really listen." This nigga was talking to me like I was his kid.

"Blaze you're my twin people so I'm going to let that one slide now don't let these words be said again."

We stepped out of the car and went into the house, they took Blaze and me to a nice looking decorated room with photos and painting of some guy in the Safari's with live and dead lions some was just in villages in Africa, I was looking at the pictures when I heard a women's voice with an accent.

"That man right there has done so much and has bought so much love and respect to a lot of people. That is until the day he raised his hands at me."

"So what's the collage for?"

"To remind me, no matter how sweet and kind some people can be there's always a monster some place lingering around the corner trying to be seen. Follow me"

We walked the halls to wherever it was we were going I watched her movements the way she moved her steps was strong and powerful I couldn't lie she was lit, the way the light hit off her chocolate complexion, she looked like a goddess her small pouty lips she had hair going back in a thick twist she had that model look not to mention her body which was amazing she had wet dream body like that Tichina Arnold Pam from Martin body, she was talking to Blaze while taking us downstairs, after she punched in a code and when the door opened I couldn't believe it she had a chemist lab, the whole science team was down here.

"Do you know why all those bosses and so called made men" she said hyphenating sign "always gotten fucked up? They only had one plan, you see me and Nora have a plan if you look me up on the net you'll find that I'm one of the best perfume moguls out here but what they don't know is this"

It was a hidden door, when she opened it and we walked in it was another lab but this was my kind of science laboratory I looked at her a little different this was somebody I needed to know, one of her people gave her a Gucci duffle bag she handed me the bag and said.

"People only know who and what you show. You're the one who would make your future strong or weak"

We been handling business out here Blaze was on call looking at me the whole conversation when he hung up he came over and said.

"We have to get back" he said with a stern look in his eyes like something wasn't on point out there in my City.

After we got finish with business we had to get out of here, Blaze told me about what's going on and when I heard what was said I just stayed quiet and waited for this flight to be over.

"They said the plane is ready" Moe said placing her phone back on her holster, she was quiet the whole trip almost forgot she was here

We got to the plane once we got there it was a few uniformed police, Blaze got out and went to the back took out something from the trunk than went to the cops with a black case he gave it to them then screamed for us.

"Come on lets go" after we boarded the plane with two uniformed police and all of our shit going back home.

Chapter 12

Nora

Twin got back with Blaze and the rest of the team. Moe was holding the bag when they all arrived, we was under the Randall Island Bridge with this old bitch begging us for her life.

"Look I had a nephew as you heard I said had, but thanks to your son Sonny I don't" while saying this I seen twin walking over to us with his gun in his hand "You see now thing's about to get real strange for you"

James was in the shadows walking like death, he stopped under the light, and he was in front of the bitch.

"Really I respect my adults, but in this case I'm going to disrespect the fuck out of you" he said.

I watched while my twin placed fear in this bitch eyes, Moe and I went to talk about everything that went down in Cali my twin had one of his girls Toni show her that this shit wasn't a game, she was on her knees with her arms tied behind her back getting stomped out like she was a young nigga that robbed one of our lounges.

"Look if you want this to stop. Tell us where your son is. Than you can go home to bed" James said.

I couldn't take the bitch cries and all of her begging. I went over and stopped them I asked my twin looking down at her.

"If you was to find out somebody done this to mommy up. What would you do?"

"I'm coming back and this shit is going down."

"Exactly, let the bitch go we'll get him. We need to talk about something else. Let's go"

We got in our cars leaving the bitch right there with the rats I took her I.D hoping she'll make that police trip. We was on our way to Harlem going to my night club my twin car was behind me, I wondered how come he didn't recognized her but my biggest concern was have he decided to make New York our empire, we had all we needed to make it happen, as we drove down 125th I looked and remembered back when I used to come out here with my girls before all the dumb smart choices I made and robbed mother fuckers out here as I drove I seen a few familiar faces and the looks that was in their eyes was sad but the hurt was when I seen my girl Veronica, she was one of my smartest girls but what I seen sitting on that cold pavement showed me even the smartest mother fucker just turns out to be the most dumbest.

We got on the F.D.R heading to 33rd heading to Hudson Yard I really didn't like the area but this was the safest place for my Lounge to be so these pigs could stay off our back.

Cutting down 31st and 1st I seen an old bodega I used to run in hiding from cops I stopped my car doubled park and got out twin done the same and stood by my side I looked at him and said.

"I need you to meet somebody. You're going to need this person on your side"

"What?" he asked surprised by what I said "Look my corners; and all of my business along with the people that's in them are all doing good sis." He had that look in his eyes like he thought I was questioning him.

"Shut up boy" I said smacking him up the head glad to have m twin in my corner.

"Bitch" he responded to my playful actions.

When we stepped in the store Mr. Rodriguez wasn't anywhere to be seen but his wife was at the counter, she looked up and placed a huge smile on her face.

"Hey. My little star Nora My sweet angel"

"Mama Rodriguez. How have you been? Is papa around?" when I said that she put on a face that told me one thing.

"Poppas gone love, three months ago those bums came in here they robbed and shot him for no reason" I didn't like what I was hearing I gave her a hug, she was shaking I let her go I really didn't know what to say so I gave her some money and my number and told her.

"I don't care where you're at or who they're with, if you ever see them again give me a call "

We all left and gotten back in our cars than pulled off, damn pops was like another father to everybody's kid or maybe a great uncle and for one of those little bastards had the nerve to kill him was fucked up.

The Lounge was doing well tonight when I stepped out my car my security Leon came over to me with his angelic smile.

"Hello ma'am"

"Stop with all that ma'am shit. How's my spot doing?"

I've gotten this idea from the Brooklyn mayor Jay Z when he opened the doors to his forty-forty club which was a smart move, when I stepped inside the scene was marvelous mother fuckers having the time of their lives on the floor, at the bar V.I.P the place was lit, money was being made. I took my twin to my office walking pass these people always made me feel like I was the top bitch, (which I was). We got to my office, I loved the way shit was moving and now that I have my other half we're going to shut this fucking City down.

Chapter 13

James

We reached twins spot, I couldn't believe what I was seeing we walked in and I almost lost my breath, this place was on point I watched while my twin handled her business, she took us to her office when she opened the door the place looked like a a new York apartment room but only much better red and black plush rug with a black scorpion tail white leather sectional sofa she had a bar with her own bartender and waiter she had a wall model T.V that let her keep her eyes on her money, my twin was large, this is the life I wanted for me and my family she told the bartender to bring us something to drink. Kiss and I went and sat, I studied my and my twin walked like she was smart, she moved like a boss, I looked at twin and asked while sipping my drink.

"So twin what's this about?"

"It's about this" she said opening the duffle bag which was full gold bricks with a black scorpion stinger print on them, she took out one "Look I wouldn't ask or have you to do shit to put you in some shit"

"I beg a differ"

"What's that supposed to mean?" she asked playfully

"Look since we linked back up a few mother fuckers haven't been back home. So yes it would be some shit; but it would be some fun shit"

My twin was going on about how well her brain was, I looked at the situation and thought about it but before coming up with a definite answer my cell started blowing up when I seen who it was I quickly answered.

"Talk to me Reign"

"Yo come out to Jersey, I'm looking at this nigga right now." After she said that I looked and said

"We have to go now"

"Why?" twin asked

"Reign said that she's looking at your friend"

"Let's go" twin said than she made sense of what was said next "No you go and take care of it, but bring his ass back here. Call Vasquez bring him with you"

"For what The dudes a cop" I responded not liking the idea.

"Look bring him trust me he's good people. You're going out to Jersey you'll need him. Now go get him"

Nora was basically the smartest of us all so questioning her nobody done, we all left my twin stayed back we got out and when we got in our cars we was gone before pulling off I told my wife that I loved her,

While driving I put on some music.

Once we all got to Jersey it was close to 12 in the morning and went out to Newark I called Reign.

"We're out here"

"Okay come out to Forest Hills, he's at this bitch spot"

"Bet" was all I said

I called Bang to let him know our destination, I rubbed the cold steel that was resting in the passenger seat thinking to myself another name has to be erased out the life book, I left Vasquez a message on where to meet us.

We got to Forest Hills and dove to Clifton Ave I never been out here and the scene is the family way of life, I seen Reign's grey Lexus parked when I pulled up beside her.

"Which house is it?" I asked

"That one right over there the brown and white family brick," I went over to Vasquez and told him what to do.

As soon as he went to ring the bell we all got out of our car's being the time it was there was nobody out. We seen the door open and some gorgeous Selena Gomez looking chic appeared, Vasquez done his part one of the females that came was walking beside me once we had that window we made our move, Vasquez took his gun out and aimed it at her face and placed his finger over his mouth when she seen how much mother fuckers was coming in her house and all the guns she seen she tied running but decided against it I walked over to her and asked.

"Where is he? And who else is here?"

"I..I..I don't know who or what you're talking about" she said in fear.

"Where's" as soon as I was going to say the name I heard

"Babe whose at the..?" he stopped at the top of the steps when he looked down, he was about to run until he heard that terrifying sound of the cocking of a gun.

"I wouldn't do that if I were you"

"A few of my people went up to him to bring him down to me, I looked at the girl and said.

"Today somebody that you don't know just saved you from somebody you do know." They hogged tied her she was so afraid she pissed on herself.

"Look I don't.." Noah said

"Yes I know you don't know us better yet know me but we do know who you are or at least know what you've done. You see what's going to happen is you're going to come with us with no problems, this place is too nice to get our work, so let's go"

Vasquez placed handcuffs on him and we all walked out. Vasquez put him in back of his car we all got in our cars and pulled off.

Driving back to New York all I was thinking about was what the fuck is going to happen to that bitch I know how this Sonny mother fucker is going to die slow and in a lot of pain, well one down and one to go, I put on some music it was too quiet and how I was feeling I wanted to have some fun, I called Vasquez and told him to find a spot so I can get this off my head.

Once we seen the bus depot we pulled up and we to the shadows Vasquez took him out the car I got out and went to get my tire iron while walking towards him making the metal scrape the floor I got up to him.

"I'm going to break you up for the pain you caused to my twin I'm going to return that to you and more" as I spoke I hit cracking him in the leg "I'm not going to kill you now but you you're going to see pain"

We got back to the city we drove to Brooklyn Brownville where twin, Kiss, Bang, and a few of our hitters was waiting on us, I called twin.

"Where are you?" was all she said

"Coming back now"

"Good. Do you have that bitch?"

"Yeah we do"

When we reached our destination it was about four in the morning when we got to Brownsville and went to an old church that was now just a scrap I seen Nora and Kiss standing there waiting for us we all stopped and got out of our cars, Vasquez took Noah out of the car now beaten up and still handcuffed, I went over to where my twin stood Vasquez walked him over and when he seen her face he tried his best to get away.

"You see, you lied so you do know me?" I said

"Look like I said I don't know you but I do know.." I stopped him

"My twin"

Nora slowly walked over to him smiled and said in the iciest tone.

"Welcome home bitch"

I looked at what she had ready for him, there were two caskets along with freshly dug graves my twin was viscous I just want the nigga to die she wanted the niggaz to die suffering, I love the way she played.

Chapter 14

Narrator

Noah was in the bed almost in a deep sleep from getting the best fuck she has ever given him, he usually celebrates his birthday with his boys but today he needed to be loved not knowing that there was a mob coming to spoil his night.

Valerie stood up to go get a drink, she threw on her silk O-Looche negligee covering her gorgeous body, her smooth caramel complexion, her breast was amazing the way the material snuggled her flesh, she had the most pretty feet she was astonishing she walked out the bedroom leaving her sexy man laying in bed, leaving the room she heard the doorbell ring not knowing what was on the other side she went to open the door and when she did she was shock from what she saw.

"What the fuck" was all she could say when she seen a police standing there "Um hello can I help you?" she said nervously.

"Is there a Noah Blake here?" she knew he was but why was they here for him so she was going to do what any girl would do at this moment

"Um no he's.." as soon as she said that Noah stood at the top of the steps.

"Babe whose at th.." as soon as those words was coming out of his mouth he seen a mob of mother fuckers barging in the house unarmed and naked he tried running to his closest gun but stopped when he heard the metallic sound followed with.

"I wouldn't do that if I was you" one of the guys said that's when three of his team came up to get him.

Noah looked at the guy with fear not understanding what was happening because he never seen none of these faces.

"Look I..I don't."

"Know who we are, better yet know who I am" the guy said to Noah.

While James told Noah of his fucked up action everybody else just ransacked the house, Vasquez placed handcuffs on Noah and they all left all accept for three girls that came who were now surrounding Valerie, as soon as the last person left they all attacked first ripping off her negligee displaying her lovely body one of them said to her

"Look we know who he is so I'm going to ask you something, now what you tell me determines if you stop your alarm tomorrow."

"Um o...o. okay whatever you want. Please don't kill me!?"

On the drive back Noah didn't have a clue on what was happening to his life so he tried getting some information.

"Look I know he's paying you but I swear you give me a call and whatever he's given you I can have you to fall back for the rest of your life" Vasquez just ignored him.

"Okay if you don't want to let me get a call, just let me know. What the fuck is I here for?" Vasquez laughed at Noah who just a week before this him and two of his boys beat and raped one of his rivals sixteen year old niece; but Noah hadn't known that this didn't have nothing to do with that, he was getting aggravated when the car came to a stop. Vasquez got a call and all he said was okay then he looked back and said.

"You're about to find out" Vasquez stop at the bus depot and drove to a far dark corner once out the car he seen one of the guy walking towards him hitting the ground with something metal, when he reached he looked at Noah and said while swinging the tire iron across Noah's leg.

"The pain I'm getting ready to bring you up on for the pain you caused my twin I'm going to return it and more, but I'm not going to kill you trust me you're about to see what pain is"

After James was done they placed Noah back in the car and continued their journey. While driving Vasquez has gotten a call and the only words that was being said was yeah okay's and sure, Noah's heart begun to rapidly he tried remembering all the fucked up shit he done. Noah had realized this ride wasn't going to a precinct but driving to the City heading towards Brooklyn he began wondering what have he done out there.

"Why are we going out here? C'mon man talk to me please. What the fuck have I done?!" Noah asked close to tears.

The four girls watched and smiled at their work as Valerie tried crawling to the door her face was bloody her left eye close shut her nose looked like the wrong sneeze would make it fall right off she had sneakers and boot prints all over her broken beaten up body tears fell from her eyes when she seen the black O-Looche boots she known was kicking her in the face earlier when she looked up she was looking down the dark hole of a gun, she knew what her next bed was going to be placed, she took that last breath she knew her life was over she closed her eyes while three hot bullets pierced through her face, they cleaned all their DNA up took what they wanted leaving Valerie's lifeless body on the floor they put the slam lock on than left jumping in their car not knowing that the neighbor has taken the description of the car down. They pulled off knowing where the family was going, than the girls went to get rid of the cars.

As soon as they took Noah out the car and walked him over to where Kiss and Nora stood when he seen the face of the woman standing there he automatically knew what this was about Nora walked over to Noah smiled and said in the iciest tone.

"Welcome home bitch"

"You see you lied to me. You do know me" James said

"I know her she's"

"My twin"

Nora opened the lock off the old rusty chain and they walked Noah to his final place, when he seen where they were taking him it was two white coffins in freshly dug graves still handcuffed Noah gave begging one last try Nora pushed him back in one of the coffins before closing the lid Nora said.

"Unlike you, you just murdered my girl, but me I want you to know when death is right there and you can't do shit about it; but don't worry you'll be having some company real soon,"

Once she had Noah where she wanted him, Nora gave orders to close the lid and have God deal with him.

It took them an hour to have Noah to be placed in his resting place. Once the job was done everyone left the lot and jumped in their cars, the sun was trying to find its way out, when they pulled off Nora which was in lead called James when he answered Nora said.

"Now let's make this Sonny mother fucker just sees darkness"

Chapter 15

James

It's been three months since that Noah shit and the weather had begin changing, my twin and I had a birthday coming up, money was coming rapidly Nora had me and Blaze around one another being that she's been seeing this dude, I like seeing my twin happy but it was something about this dude that I didn't like, it was like I seen his face from somewhere, Blaze and I was checking on a money situation, we were driving Blazes ivory and powder blue pathfinder heading to Queens, my wife face timed me.

"Hey my goddess, I'm type busy. What's going on?" I asked

"Babe I want you to sit down."

"I'm driving. What's up?"

"Babe what are we missing? The two of us that is" she asked.

"Can we please get to it?"

"We're pregnant babe"

My wife and I spoke I, was stuck listening while she and Nora laughed over the news, I was thinking about what happened to my first born and how I wasn't there for those short few months of his life they tried getting my attention

"Yeah I'm still here" than I said "This nigga has to die"

"Did you hear what I just said?" she asked close to tears.

"Yes did you? Look queen I'm more than happy but facts is facts and you know as well as he does, his time is near"

We spoke for a little more than I hung up. Blaze and I reached Queens and got to Jackson Heights where we was to meet up with one of our peoples who seems like they dropped out of school or at least forgotten how to do math. We seen the only money green Bentley so I knew this nigga was close, I got out and as soon as I looked up I seen the nigga in the Barber Shop Blaze and myself walked in and all the talking came to a stop, Al Greene was playing and as we walked over to Mike I seen fear in some of their eyes, we had a few of our people outside just in case shit was to get filthy. I sat in the vacant seat next to his he was now getting a shape up blaze threw on a barber's coat I looked around and said.

"Please everybody just continue on your day" then I looked at Mike reflection in the mirror and said "So Mike you know you're in some shit right?"

"Look I messed up Jay I promise I'll get you and Nora the mon.." I said stopping him from saying his bullshit.

"Look you really think that I'm here for a little change? Oh no we have money and a lot of it this is more about you and your dumbass actions" Blaze looked at everybody and said to a kid.

"Lil man I want you to get everybody I.D and phones and bring them even your daddies if you happen to forget one then he won't be the only one in trouble" than I said to everybody else in the Barber Shop.

"Everybody here will be leaving all except Mr. Mike, if any of you decide to feel sorry for Mike you will have a visitor, a visitor neither one of you would want to see"

Once I gotten all the shit we sent everybody out, once the last body was out we went to business,

"Mike help me understand this? We hand you 24 kilos of the best shit you can get your fucked up hands on and all we asked you to do was make sure our money don't come up short. Now why is it that every time we go in your kitchen your pots doesn't look right?"

We walked him to the office and sat him at the bosses' desk and we sat across from him and Blaze asked.

"So boss tell me what should we do with this Mike guy?" than I said

"Should we handle him our way?" then I put the most serious look and said "Let's get to business. Put your hands up here" I said aiming at the desk.

Mike had placed his hands on top of the desk, that's when Blaze and myself took out our guns placed the muzzle on both of his hands and without another thought we both shot him in the hands while he screamed in agony blood leaking from his hands.

"Put your hands on the desk, or die your call" Blaze said sharply, once Mike has done what was told we both took out our army knives out took hold of his wrist and begun digging the knives into the bullet hole, and said

"You're going to remember being stupid. My twin let you in trusted you fed and dressed you and what you do is you still from us. No we're not going to kill you Mike we're family but I swear what your life is about to become you're going to kill yourself."

Blaze and I left him in the office in pain leaking blood from both hands, I called Boe who was waiting outside once he opened the gate we left closing that nigga in. I liked teaming up with Blaze his energy was like mine and that was to never give a fuck, we left the keys got in our cars and pulled off I called twin to let her know that was taking care of once that call was done I called my boy Bang who was now with this nigga Mikes wife being that she only trusted Bang out of everybody else we sent him, his phone rung twice until I heard

"Yo Jay what's good?"

"It's done we're going to link up with Nora" after that was done we headed to the lounge.

Chapter 16

Bang

I looked at her while she sat across the table from me, she was gorgeous dark chocolate complexion, she looked like she had that get out of the water glow like she just shines under the sunlight she was a grown women with that young lady look, her lips was luscious her small button nose she looked like that actress Tika Sumpter but she had that Tracy Ellis body I mean really she was bad everything about her was labeled IT from her come fuck me eyes to her lovely lips but no matter how bad she was business was being taking care of. James called and told me that everything was handled with, I looked at Melissa took her by the hand and said.

"I just got a call th..." she stopped me from talking.

"I know you have to go" she said with a disappointed look on her face

"What's that for?" I asked

We spoke for a little more than I left the restaurant leaving her alone at the table. When I stepped outside the cool breeze smacked me in the face I looked up and seen a few cop cars I casually walked and got in my car while one of their eyes was focused on me I just put on some (Nipsey Hussle) and pulled off.

While I drove the area and looked at the individuals and remembered the nights my pops was out here, him and my uncle was two of the most feared mother fuckers in Harlem until death came knocking, my pops died while cheating on my mom's while she was on her death bed some people say that the bitch had set him up one of the families that they had war with ran in the hotel and just shot my father 20 times he was done so bad my mother had to have a closed casket, they got my uncle and aunt and some of their team at my pops funeral and once that happened they empire collapsed and at that time I was too young to pick it up so I just went and created my own situation. I had a team throughout Brooklyn and Queens for years until I met Blue as soon as we connected that was it.

Money, chic's, finest clothes everything we needed we had, I missed my boy, but now I have Nora who is basically the realest partner that I have ever had.

I called my wife, we was going through our shit she was mad at me for her cheating on me but I still loved her, she wanted a baby don't get me wrong yes I wanted one also but now wasn't the time, when she didn't answer I hung up I was at the red light when a cop car pulled up alongside of mine I looked and noticed it was that cop from earlier once the light turned green I pulled off they done the same tailing behind me thinking I was going to speed from their bullshit scare tactics when I stayed on the speed limit they went pass me dumb motherfuckers maybe they was trying to scare me or not but whichever one it was fuck it.

I was going into B.K heading to check out the Barkley Center she wanted to buy out that arena for their birthday. Nora wanted their day to be a blast and nobody but her would do something like buy out the arena for the night, I had to meet up with the owner to pay him off one thing about Nora was she wanted these motherfuckers to know with her it's straight money, no bouncing checks or pin codes etc James was my nigga unlike his twin he's the street nigga that like to do shit by cards and checks. I reached Atlantic and the site wasn't anything like I remembered back when only real niggaz was out, quiet niggaz knew their place, and if you were a bitch than the house was always the place for you, but nowadays it's a whole different situation.

I parked in front of the arena got out and went for the money, when I stepped in and gave him a call,

"Brian my man Where are you?" he said in the blackest whitest voice you can here.

"In the lobby"

"Come up to my suite"

I got on the elevator and there was one of those idiot boys on it. I shook my head

"Owners suite please" it was smooth elevator music being played. When the door opened and I seen the room I damn near lost my breath this shit was laced this shit looked better than a lot of apartments I seen, the owner was sitting on his black and white leather sofa that was in the far corner the man had a fucking bed in his office, he had a female in the office with him she looked like a wannabe lawyer but she was gorgeous but I wasn't here for her

"Brian Big Bang my man! Would you like drink?" he asked

"Nah I'm good let's just take care of this"

"Yes the business. You need the Arena. Am I right?"

After taking care of business I stood up to leave he said some fake friend business bullshit I just shook my head than left the scene I got back on the elevator going down I called Nora and let her know she had the arena, when I got outside the rain was pouring while jumping in my ride something had hit me all this getting money shit that we been doing I needed to call my girl Laydee.

"Hey big daddy, you finally called a bitch huh?" she asked

"Where you're at babe?"

"I'm at Kayla's on Valentine"

"Okay I'm coming now"

I sat in my car waiting for a few seconds than I pulled off, I use to want to fuck with Kayla but she was so stuck on this small time hustling dude and at that time Kayla was everything men dream about fucking and every women try being, she had that step out of the water model body, caramel complexion, she kept her hair laced shit if she wasn't so stuck on dude I probably would've pulled a Jay Z and put a rock on her hand, I stopped at the red light and called Laydee and told her where to be the phone rang only one time when I heard

"Yes big daddy" she said sounding like she was ready for Big Bang

"Better yet babe's meet me at my spot. You still have the keys right?"

"I'm still with Kayla I'm leaving now."

Once I got to the Bronx I quickly drove home I really didn't like the neighborhood I was now living but in every man life no matter who he is, has to grow up so I bought this house out in Throgs Neck (had to leave the Projects.)

I got to my house on Quincy street when I pulled up I noticed Laydee's Porsche parked in my driveway while the rain still poured she stepped out of the car and although the sky was grey she looked like sunshine, I got out not worrying about the rain we just stood there in one another's arms, she pressed her body onto mine allowing me to an automatic hard-on she was a little bold placing her hand down my pants and went straight for my bat and started caressing it, I took her by the hand and went straight for my house, as soon as she got me behind the door she went for me burying her tongue down my throat, she stepped back and started disrobing when she took off her O-Looche trench coat and when I seen what was under all I could've done was lick my lips and I went right for her she had on her O-Looche tight fit black jeans that hugged her thighs and boosted her lovely ass she wore a strawberry spaghetti top blouse, I quickly took off her top and oh my god shed had the best set of succulent breast a man can ever see on a queen, she took off her lace front bra allowing her now hard heresy shaped nipples to been shown, we kissed our way to the living room I pushed her back on my Artisan sofa.

sectional sofa I put on some music from my McIntosh MXA80 Integrated audio system that Kelly Rowland Motivation remix with Busta Rhymes, Trey Songz, Da Brat etc came on I quickly took off her pants all the while having her thongs to also come off once I got a look at her full body my boy began to rise harder ready to work so I undressed I wasn't going to rush this time so I buried my face between her thigh's softly kissing my way down to her spot as soon as I reached I started kissing her now swollen lips sliding my tongue inside of her love glove her body begun to jerk and shudder her moans was sexy her groan was like porn I started fucking her with my tongue stopped for a second and looked down on her and at that moment I didn't even care- about her not reciprocating I slowly slid my shaft inside of her now hot wet sex while penetrating her with the music playing it was like we was dancing while fucking my rhythm was matched with every beat and sound of the song I turned her around and entered her from behind while fucking her I looked down and my black dick was all white covered in her juices my thrust and pounds has gotten harder and faster and much deeper her moans was getting louder.

"Yess daddy fuck this pussy mmm" she said as I started getting close to that time I started giving her that D.MX Belly fucking I felt myself getting real close to reaching I gave a few more hard thrust than pulled out and blast my seed over her ass after I was done I fell down on top of her, we laid there on the sofa in each other's hold covered in sweat and just fell out.

Chapter 17

James

Life's been looking good for me since I've walked out of those prison doors, I found my twin and my mother, my wife is giving me another chance at becoming a father and this money was coming in like rain on a stormy day. Nora was mover and a real money maker she was truly a boss, the way how thing's was going was great New York was ours if money was to be made from other motherfuckers they had to come through us we was the source to everything out here nothing moved unless we gave an okay, I was in one of our Scorpion Sting Clubs in the office looking over our numbers when I looked up and seen on the security cam and what I seen made me react like a cat when I seen that we had some unwanted guest, I quickly got up and went to see what was they doing in my place. When I got out to the front there was fucking cops all in my shit.

"May I help you with something?" I asked the lead officer

"We're looking for Nora Lee" the female officer said

"What the fuck for? Matter of fact fuck that" I took out my lawyers card and gave it to them "You have to ask anything about any Lee's here's our Lawyer's card give her a ring. Now can you and all of your seat warmers get the hell out of my establishment?

They tried that power trip shit but once they seen that I wasn't backing down they all left, I called my twin she just laughed and said "So" when we hung up I went back to the office to continue what I was doing, going over the books I came across a situation. Nora was out with her boy toy following her around I been had a bad feeling about the nigga but she liked the bitch so I just fell back until he proves me right, then I'll really introduce myself to him but then again if he do I'm sure twin will make me miss the party. Twin was smart and I know she can handle herself, I looked at our number's and smiled at what I was looking at Nora was a genius we was making a killing whatever had our logo if we opened a door we had money coming in.

We had our big 3 0 and she wanted to have a bash I was making sure of it that all of our shooters know their position, Twin said that she didn't want or need any security but I wasn't stupid, we done did too much shit and that was only when we got back together and I wasn't thinking about what we done alone.

One of our spots was for the night so twin, Blaze, and myself wanted our people to meet up cause she wanted everybody to know how she wanted things to be that night, I went to place the books back in the safe, my twin had all the money this club and one of our Lounges money was in this safe.

I left for two days I called her, being that she was pregnant I didn't want or need her out here so she stayed home taking care of our profits.

"Hey my love" she said as she answered

"I'm about to be done, on my way home now."

We hung up I was walking out the doors of the club and when I got outside I smiled at what I went through, a great stick up kid to becoming one of the scariest names in New York City I got in my car put on a new joint from one of those young rappers out the Bronx called Slime Tyme while driving I was about to call twin when I seen one of my workers but what I seen next was crazy I seen my twins lil puppy boy with him walking out of a Bodega I really didn't want to think the wrong shit being that it looked to be nothing important so I just said fuck it, I pulled off I wanted to call twin but knowing her she probably done her back ground on the nigga I just hopped she didn't just go for the pretty face and boyish smile.

I got to the Bronx going home, I needed to change. Looking at these little hustlers and schemers I smirked at the thought of when I came from, the shelters, homes, jails, and the streets, now I got a queen small castle and soon to be having my lil prince or princess shit was looking real good for a nigga who has lost a lot just to gain so fucking much; but out of everything I got the one thing I really want is my son and my pops (well more like my pops).

Once I got home I noticed my wife's platinum Benz, in the dive-way I parked behind hers and got out when I went inside the first thing I done was called out for my wife when she hadn't responded I went for my gun but when she walked out from the studies she had on a O-Looche negligee I had custom made for her and she looked radiant as I stood there looking at my wife I started to think, this was what I've been missing all those years this is what I'm doing this shit for.

"Hey my young black middle class rich husband" my wife said giving me a kiss I looked at my wife and said.

"Don't be so comfortable cause those people always have to worry about something I don't want us in that type of class"

We went to the back where we had a scorpion shape pool an oak wood deck everything a man need was here and although we have neighbors the scenery looked amazing I was behind my wife hugging her from the stomach and said.

"We came far and I wouldn't want to be in that car with no other woman but you. We have one last situation as soon as that's done we can rest"

Chapter 18

Narrator

He was sitting in his mother's hospital room looking down on her now pale sick face while looking at flyer for a birthday bash and when he seen who the party it was for he put on a devilish smile he looked down as his mother laid in the hospital bed being supported by the respirator he knelt down looking at her now pale skin and said.

"I swear to you the both of those bastards are going to join you real soon" once he said those words that's when he heard that terrible sound from that horrible machine he let out a slight tear covered his mother's face than he left the room, while leaving the room he looked at the flyer before placing the flyer back in his pocket he swore to himself while mouthing the words.

"Y'all motherfuckers time is coming real soon"

Sonny didn't know there were two to deal with he had already known how treacherous James was but the girl he knows nothing of he walked out the double doors of the hospital thinking.

How bad can this one girl be? He jumped in his black pathfinder put on an old classic from one of the greats Tu-Pac and listened to the song "Dear Mama" and pulled off while driving to his new young ladies house to try to put his plan together. Sonny knew going against James alone was a problem now he sees that it's another one to have to deal with, and since he had done his fucked up shit his team hadn't approved of and they all turned their backs on him which had forced his hand to place them in their resting place. He still had three trusted shooters still on his side.

He reached Saint Nicolas projects in Manhattan and double parked once he jumped out he phoned Jessica when she answered she had Salsa playing in the background she answered him in a sexy.

"Yes Pa-pi"

"Down stairs buzz the door"

Bags was at the counter purchasing a pack of New Ports, while the undercover was walking behind him reminding him of all the shit they had on him, as he walked out of the Bodega Bags stopped to light up a smoke, while the two men stood there talking not knowing that the worst pair of eyes was now watching them.

"Look you fucking asshole, we have so much shit on you motherfucker, your whole damn fam..." Bags stopped him from talking

"If you had anything worth wild we wouldn't be having this conversation. Besides aren't you fucking her? Why don't you..." before he could've finished what he was going to say he found himself with a nickel plated 357 in his face.

"Go ahead why don't I what? Finish it"

"Noting, you got it, nothing" Bags said with his hands up

"That's what I thought"

The two men stood back up straight and continued their conversation Bags couldn't believe what he has gotten himself into, the undercover tried scaring Bags into getting all the info he needed, Bags looked him into his cold eyes and thought about his options. He wanted any information on certain individuals who got found without breathing. Mike has been after Nora for a while and now he's close to his promotion (so he thought) Bags looked at Mike and said.

"Look you have us all wrong sir. We are all church going people"

"You think this shit's a game. Don't you?"

Bags was ready for whatever's about to come towards him Bags was willing to lay down his life for Nora so being behind a cell wasn't shit to the young 21 year old, at this moment Bags could've seen that he was getting Mike upset he just laughed at him and walked away Mike was pissed he was just about to follow Bags but his phone stopped him, he smiled when he seen the name on the phone.

"Hello gorgeous. What you're up to?" he asked whomever he was talking too.

"I'm just working almost done if you want to meet up"

While Sonny was sitting in Jessica's kitchen puffing on a freshly rolled blunt his mind was doing cartwheels in his head, he looked at the flyer having his eyes to get even redder Jessica walked over to him taking the flyer out of his hand and guided him towards the bedroom she playfully pushed Sonny back on her comfortable hybrid mattress and started getting undress as done what she was doing Sonny had started doing the same, once the both of was birthday suited ready Jessica went down to grab hold of Sonny's now erect member aimed straight up ready for her to do as she pleased Jessica took his manhood and securely placing him in her tight grasp and placed him in her mouth slowly going down on his shaft allowing her pillow plumped lips warm up shaft the feeling felt so good his toes began having a mind of its own, she stood up and slowly climbed on top of his pole once he was fully inside of her wet world his eyes was shut as he clinched his teeth as she rode him slowly going up but forcefully going down she eased her gyrations looking him in his eyes she had Sonny in her world her moans and groans sounded so beautiful Sonny was in total bliss they both began going at each other like a pair of cats in heat Sonny took Jessica by the waist tuned her over she looked back at her man placed one hand on his muscular chest while the other held on the headboard she told her lover in the sexiest Latinas voice.

"Papi give it to me. Fuck me big daddy" Sonny grabbed hold of her long black silky hair and entered her from behind, her pussy was so wet Sonny's manhood slipped out a few times, his thrust and pound begun getting vigorous her moans was getting louder and since they were on the second floor they knew people had definitely heard them the headboard was hitting the wall, Sonny had closed his eyes and seen the two faces he hate all of a sudden he begun going harder and faster, the session was good and he felt himself getting to that point he looked down at his member proud of what he seen that was covered all over it he gave a few more hard thrust he was cuming and he wasn't going to move out yet when he reached Sonny released all his juice inside of her.

Bags was in an U-ber going to wherever Nora needed him to be, she told him she had something for him the first thing that came to his mind was that he's about to go home he stated thinking about the meetings he was having with Mike or was it the fact that he's been fucking a few of her workers, lately Bags been on a fuck up spree he thought while sitting in the back seat Bags mind was now racing and fear begun to take over his vision the female driver put on some music when she turned on 55th and 3rd Bang knew his drive was coming to a stop once he noticed Nora's gold range rover parked when the driver came to a stop his heart rate began to speed as he paid for the ride.

Once bags went inside the restaurant he seen Nora and a few of the family Bags walked to the back where everybody was sitting scared as he gotten closer Boe stood up and Bags begun sweating Nora took a sip of her drink and asked.

"How have you gotten here?"

"An U-ber. Why you ask?" Bags asked relived by the question

"Well I have something for you" they all went to the back of the restaurant where there was an ivory and red range rover sport HSE

"I don't want you or anybody else in this family walking or use public transportation" Nora said

They all went back in the restaurant where it was now empty they all sat and Nora begun

"We are now and always will be a dominant but smart Empire, whatever comes through this City it comes through us…" James interrupted

"Look, fuck all this we run shit bullshit speech. The reason why she have you all here is to put everybody in line I'm not saying that she's mothering y'all" James said.

James had a different way of doing things which Nora didn't approve of but neither of them wanted to look bigger than the next in front of their people so Nora just got up from her seat James went behind her

"Look I know that you're mad but my job is to make sure that you always make it back home. You want this going out everywhere like we haven't done shit out here.."

"You sound like you're scared"

"No not scared I'm just not that stupid " James spat back Nora was getting real pissed but held her cool in front of outsiders so fighting in front of individuals none of them was going to do. Before leaving without looking back to face her twin she said.

"I know you're head is on you just better hope that nothing goes wrong." after saying that three of her close shooters walked out with her, when they got outside they jumped in her range rover and pulled off.

Chapter 19

James

Night of hell

Twin and my birthday arrived and everything was going as planned, we bought out the Nets arena, everybody was in here, twin and I had every big name, hustlers, whomever was somebody was here, I wanted this to be a loud fun quiet night but whenever a bunch of high egos and fake bosses are in one spot something's bound to happen, twin and I was in V.I.P sitting on thrones like the royalty we are, I had a couple of young rappers from Bronx and Brooklyn in here,

I wanted our mother here but twin said no, for most of the night everything was going good until a Jamaican female came in with three Jamaican guys the dumb bitch had a bullhorn calling out a name while my team went towards them her fake need to be heard Jamaican niggaz had pulled out their guns she looked at twin and said.

"You really should listen when people speak to you," she said in her Island voice "I tell you me niece she bedda be safe" I didn't know the bitch, I had my toy in my hand when I looked at my twin she was saying no, but me this was my type of play, as soon as I was about to let my little big man speak I noticed Bang and my girl Kim getting close to them and once Kim was in place with no hesitation she had her gun aimed at the back of the stupid bitch head and as soon as the dumb ass was quiet and most importantly gun less my twin and I had got to where she and her team was I seen that this chic had no type of sense she looked at me and said sounding like she look.

"Do you have an idea who the fuck I am?"

"Yes a dead dread. I'm not one of the wisest, but I do believe that if you or these assholes you have here really wanted to do something about whatever had happened you would've picked another day and time. Look around this is already in the media" I said than I aimed my gun at them, they decided to just leave the shit to see another day.

For the rest of the night we all went on partying Nora and I was sitting in V.I.P. while everybody else was having fun I noticed that nigga of hers walking in the place like this was his shit, it was weird how he begun talking to motherfuckers like he known them personally I kept my eyes on him all the way until he done the next hand shake to someone which told me who the nigga was. Nora hadn't seen it I walked on the dance floor and went over to Bang and Blaze and had let them know about what I just had seen; I didn't want to mess this night up so I just kept it to myself.

I knew there was something about this dude I didn't like and there it was, he was talking to twin giving her his fake ass gift Kiss got on the mic and said while looking at me.

"Baby I know you told me not to get you anything but since I've known you, you've always listened to this one woman and since I can't sing Happy Birthday to you my king."

When I heard the keys to a Baldwin BP165 piano and then heard the voice of my favorite female singer's she sung to me and twin, although it was one of the best things anybody has done for me my attention was on this Mike character he was playing twin too close than I remembered seeing Bags and him talking I went to get Blaze and a few more of our people and went to get some answers, when I reached him he was talking to some thick chocolate sexy chic I looked at him and said with hate in my eyes.

"We need to talk" I said to him.

"Okay let me.." he responded trying to brush me off.

"Bags I said we need to talk" I guess he seen that this wasn't a complementary meeting. We went to a secluded spot in the arena. I looked him in the eyes and said "Bags I'm going to ask this but once and please don't fuck around. Who is this Mike dude?" we all had our guns out "Please be smart cause I seen you when you thought you was being cautious. Now I asked a question"

"Isn't he with your twin? I don't…" we all cocked our guns than opened his eyes wide.

"Think again." I said with death in my eyes.

"Okay ok listen the nigga got me trapped and I can't get out"

"So what you're saying is that he's K9?"

"Yes that's what I'm saying" Bags said still with that fear look in his eyes.

"Do my twin know this?" as soon as he was about to answer Nora came and broke up our get together.

"Is this only my birthday?" she asked.

"Nah we're coming now" I looked at my twin and asked

"Before going back let me know. How much you know about this nigga you're with?"

"Don't you start that big brother shit cause remember I'm the oldest. Now let's go" she said grabbing hold of my hand.

When we got back out I could've sworn I seen that Sonny motherfucker but it wasn't so I placed my attention back on that nigga Mike, he was with my twin dancing, I really didn't want to mess this up for her but one thing I didn't like was a snake and besides it was me and my twins day but tomorrow is another story.

The night went on great mother fuckers was dancing having a good time until a fight between these two you tube rappers had popped off once that was done with Kiss myself and twin had left the party, as soon as we got out the cold air was whooping our ass we all rushed in our cars and pulled off.

The next day I was getting ready to go out of town and I wanted that nigga Mike to join me I knew my twin would've been mad at me but this was something I had to do, my wife was still sleeping while I was on the phone with Blaze.

"We taking that nigga Mike with us to Miami," I said to Blaze than I changed the tone in m voice "But one of us won't be coming back."

"Say less." he said than we hung up.

We was going out there to check out some new product which we really needed this connect, Kiss had woke up and begun hugging and rubbing her stomach on my back, than she asked me something I didn't need her to know.

"Where you're off too baby?" I didn't want to lie

"Going to Miami have to take care of business" I said afraid of her next question "Have to meet up with a new product"

"Want me to come with you?"

"Nah taking Blaze and Mike" I gave her a kiss than I left.

I got outside and got in my Black Benz I had both of our guns with me with the duffle bag of money I called my boy Bang when he picked up he sounded like he was getting some morning fun.

"Yo Bee I need you to watch over my spot while I'm gone"

"You're doing that Miami trip?" he asked.

"Yeah bro and I need to holla at you before I go too"

"What's popping big homie."

"Yo meet up with me at the spot it's important"

"Bet I'll be there in fifteen" he said then hung up.

We hung up and I pulled off and my mind was on what Bags said I called Nora but she didn't pick up.

I was on my way to meet up with Blaze and Bang being that he didn't think I knew about his mask I also called Mike, I had too much shit running though my mind about what I should do when I heard his voice all I could think about was him placing cuffs on my twins wrist.

"Yeah Jay what's up?" he asked

"Yo Mike listen I'm taking this trip I was just wondering if you want to roll"

"What trip? And where?" he asked suspiciously.

"We're out to Miami being that you're with my twin I need to know more about you" I knew I had to do this

"Okay bet, Where we meeting up?"

"I'm sending somebody to get you now"

Once we hung up my mind was focused on my missions and taking this niggaz life had to happen. I called Lisa one of our sexy young hustlers for the job, she was basically the sexiest of all our runners she resembled a little like that Naomi chic from WWE she was bad in every way possible from the face to the body.

"Yes James" she said answering the phone. Her job was to get him there making sure he was off point while I go in and just take him out there but I had thought about something worse.

"I need you to go and pick somebody up for me and bring him to the spot on Fordham" once I told her everything to do I got up and went to go get dressed.

Once I reached the spot I seen my boys rides parked along with Lisa's and I also seen my twins ride. I really didn't need her around but fuck then I remembered that nigga Mike. I double parked and hopped out my ride, I noticed my boy Flo standing out front smoking a blunt.

It's weird that my twin has this hookah lounge that you can't smoke bud inside; I approached Flo taking a puff of his blunt and asked.

"Who's inside?" I asked walking towards the door.

"Bang, Blaze, and Lisa, with that nigga Mike."

"Good looking" I said than I went in, when I stepped inside Bang and Blaze was laughing and joking with the nigga I just looked at this motherfucker with hate and thought about all the information he must've had gotten from my twin and how much times this nigga lied to my twin. And not to mention what was his end game going to be? As I gotten closer my hate was growing and the more I thought about it the more I thought about putting a hole in this niggas head that's when Blaze said.

"Yo Jay what's good bro?" when I heard his voice I came out that short daze, I walked over to where they sat I didn't need my attention to be on the nigga so I just went straight to business.

"Look I'm going on a trip to check something out Bang you and Mike will come with me Blaze you're going stay watch over.." the nigga Mike interrupted me from what I was saying.

"You said you want me to come with you? I'm lost about that."

"You're with my twin I haven't had any time to get up with you. Is that going to be a problem?"

"Nah bro we good" he responded. I just went to get a drink and then we all just left.

We was on the plane Bang and I was talking about business I really didn't care about what he was saying my attention was focused a little on Mike being that he wasn't coming back I gave Bang a look, then the pilot said we was taking off, I don't know how high were we when I took out my two guns and Bang followed behind. We aimed them at Mike he just looked all scared.

"What the fuck!! What's going on?" Mike asked looking scared with his hands up in the air.

"I'm going to ask you a few questions Mike. And please don't lie."

"Yeah,, No problem.. Whatever man." he said looking at what was in my hands.

"Okay... Now what's your job title?" when I asked that his skin just turned dull. "By that look I think you know what my next question is?"

"Look I don't know what you're talking about but you got me all wrong Jay" I looked out the window than I looked at him and smiled. "I'm just fucking with you man. Here light this up" I passed him a laced blunt while I lit a blunt for Bang and myself. We sat there smoking like everything was good and once the nigga was out I didn't give a fuck about where we was or what was under us I told Bang to open the door once he done it I had threw the nigga out the door, I didn't know where the nigga would land and I really didn't care neither once the door closed we was on our way to Miami.

When we got to Miami I was ready to get this shit over with, Bang was on his cell I knew who he was talking to by his movements, we hoped in the two black Lexus jeeps that's been waiting for us there was three women waiting beside the jeeps.

I really didn't need us to stay out here any longer than we needed to be, the chic that was in the front of the pack came over to us.

"Hello welcome to our part of town. Should we get down to business?"

"That'll be great" I responded

We was on our way to see this new connect whose name's been roaming the streets all over New York bang was on his cell I guess talking to Nora, I looked at him while he was having his conversation than he looked at me and shook his head and said.

"Yo Jay she's asking for you" I looked at him and said

"What she talking about?"

"What you think?"

"Give me the phone" I said, he gave me his phone

"What's up twin?"

"Are y'all out there in Miami?"

"Yeah why you ask?"

"Need to know. Have you heard from Mike?"

"Nah I haven't. What's going on?"

"Nothing just take care of business"

Chapter 20

Nora

This was the best time of my life, my twin was back, my business is making a killing and I'm in a great relationship I was feeling good about being the queen of New York.

I was in my Scorpion Sting club sipping on a Long Island Iced Tea Kiss was with me with her pregnant glow I looked at her and said.

"Something isn't right"

"What's wrong? What are you talking about?"

"Mike he's always beside me or he always wake me up."

"Listen, whatever happened we'll find out; but right now we needs to focus on this money and you"

She was right I couldn't worry about Mike especially while my twin is making that move and all my people is out on these streets working and looking for this dude Sonny, it's been said that he was at my birthday bash, his life has already became shit and now it's about to turn into hell I really didn't want to keep my focus on Mike so I went to check on my money. I knew I didn't need to but my mind wasn't on my side.

"Come on girl let's go check something out"

When Kiss and I got out I seen Bags ride parked out front, when I looked up I seen him talking to some girl I called Blaze to see what was going on but his phone just rung something that never happened I tried it again and the same thing happened I didn't like this so I begun calling a few of my gunmen I didn't want to think the wrong but I also didn't need to be stupid. I called Vasquez to see if Blaze was in a cell but he didn't have any knowledge of anything. I told everybody that I called to meet me at Blaze house. I walked over to bags.

"Bags did you hear from Mike?"

"Not since the birthday. Why what happen?"

"I'm calling him but he's not picking up" when I said that he had this look on his face that told me he had some information

"What's wrong?"

"What do you know that I don't?" he didn't answer the question and anytime Bags don't answer my questions it's because he's trying not to lie to me, I left it alone and got in my car, I told my driver to take me to Blazes house; I was in my own blank world thinking about what the hell is going on.

My twin and Bang was out in Miami handling business, while we drove through these streets I thought about stepping back for a little bit and maybe have a family but then again how can I do that with my type of work.

We got to Blaze place and his car was still in his driveway okay that was a good sign. I noticed three of my shooters cars I got out and went straight to the door.

When I walked in it didn't look like anything happened I sent the team to check around I walked up his marble stone stairway and went to his room where the door was left ajar as I got closer I heard moaning when I opened the door Blaze had that girl Kaylah riding him, he looked and seen me and act like he just got caught by his mother, I went back downstairs and was on my way out the door when I heard Blaze

"I'm sorry I didn't.."

"Look go upstairs and finish up I need you focused"

I was sitting in my car waiting while I waited I started thinking about this Sonny motherfucker he thought he was low walking in my party, as I was thinking Blaze came out with that Kaylah girl she was cute like she could've been a Wild n' Out girl, Blaze gave her a kiss and got in his car, when I pulled off everybody followed behind.

When we all had reached my club before stepping out something came on the T.V

"Breaking news today there was a man came falling from the sky no one knows how but it looks as if he was thrown out a building or a plane" they hadn't said a name of the person that had got killed or committed suicide I got out and went in my club Blaze was right behind me being that my partner wasn't here I had Kiss with me I told the bartender to bring me a Long Island Iced tea when I sat down I went right to business.

"Look I don't know what my brother want to do about the situation but an enemy of his is still walking around and.."

"My husband wants him dead nothing more than that" Kiss said I looked at Blaze and said

"I need you to check on what happened to Mike something is wrong and I don't like it" bags said something I didn't get "What was that?"

"Do you know what he did for a living?"

"Why have you said did like past tense? What's going on Bags?"

"I didn't mean it like that boss. Trust me I didn't"

"When my twin gets back I want everybody on post on their spots and I want every fucking body know about Scorpion Sting."

After we got done I told Blaze to walk with me I had something else coming up I just wanted the three of us to know about. Blaze came over to me ready for whatever.

"I need you to find out what happened with Mike, I got something going on it's going to be big just waiting until my twin gets back but first get on that Mike situation"

I got in my car and told the driver to take me to Brooklyn I had to meet up with a big time hustler that been running the street of Brooklyn with my permission while we drove to Brooklyn a slight thought came to mind what if that was Mike the News was talking of today but that was just that a thought cause Mike doesn't have any problems and I know he's not out here doing him, I didn't need to keep thinking the wrong shit so I told my driver to put on some music while we drove to Brooklyn I was in my own world when my phone started ringing.

"Talk to me"

"Boss its Lou. I want you to keep your eyes open it's a word going around that somebody is trying to sleep you.." I really didn't care about what was said I just told him.

"I'm on my way now wide awoke and trust me I'm not tired yet"

When I got to Brooklyn I wasn't alone Blaze and a few of my strongest team also came along it was around four when we got to Brooklyn damn this would be the right time to have Bang and my twin with me but if there have to be a family get together then so be it we reached Clinton Hill and there were four of Lou's roughest girls securing his property Lou was a little like Bang with his money he had his eyes on every one of his dollars but unlike Bang Lou would break a finger if u came up a dollar short, I met Lou through his wife before she died she was one of the realist bitches in New York period and when I seen how he moved I had to keep him around. Although he had to pay to stay he really didn't care especially since he owned half of Brooklyn and Queens Lou was a crazy Jamaican act and dressed as such, Lou was sitting on a beach chair in the cold weather eating a tub of ice cream when he seen my car he stood up and came over to greet me

"Boss lady glad to see you" he said wanting to give me a hug.

"Go clean yourself this is a $3,500.00 coat. What's going on out here?" I asked

"Do you recall what I just told you about an hour ago?"

"Yeah yeah I don't care about that. Where's my money?"

"I have that and a bonus boss" he was the only one who always refers to me as a boss shit I didn't like it but understood. "Follow me"

Lou took us to a basement that looked as if it could've been a dungeon as we walked further I heard other voices, I looked at Blaze and noticed he had his hand on his piece when we reached to where Lou was taking us I couldn't believe who and what I was now seeing. They had the motherfucker who was walking dead, Lou said to me.

"He was going around trying to find help in coming at James but he just didn't know that he was talking to family" I looked at Sonny and said to him with a smile.

"I got your ass now. And death is right beside me" he looked at me with tears in his eyes along with a beaten up face

"I don't even know who the fuck you are I.."

"Was looking for help so you can do to my twin what you've done to his son. So that means you do know who I am, but first." I took out my phone and face timed my twin when he answered he was around Bang.

"I'm on my way back now. What's up?"

"Look who came to dinner" I said showing him the now bloody face Sonny

"That's who I think it is?"

"If you think that's the walking dead then you're right"

"Don't touch him until I get there"

"Can't promise you anything, besides your wife looks like she's about to send him to church in a box" this was getting to be one of the best days this year I looked at Sonny and said.

"I came to pick something up but right now" I said to Lou without looking back "Lou you keep that. Blaze you and Bags take his ass to the car and trunk him"

Kiss and I was with Lou watching his new opp and what he was trying to do was good but in the wrong area.

"Do you know what's over there?"

"Yes money, money that I need"

"Okay, that's cool but if you go out there than just know that you're on your own. Not even my people go out there. Think about it Lou"

He wanted to open work right across the street from a precinct and a school he was brave but also stupid, I went out to my car hearing this nigga going crazy in the trunk, I slowly walked behind my car and softly slid my hand across it saying to him.

"Today you're going to die Mr. Sonny that I promise you" I than got in my car and told my driver to take me to Brownsville finally we'll be able to put this behind us.

Chapter 21

James

We got back to New York safe with this new raw white Liquid I really didn't know what we needed more shit for when we had everything in N.Y.C on lock. Nora called me showing me that they had that faggot Sonny, I rushed to my car like nothing else mattered they was out in Brooklyn and I knew where they was going but with all this light outside I know she wasn't going to make a soul deposit knowing that motherfuckers would be out around the area, Bang was in his car behind mines we had 3 U-haul with what we brought back from Miami I called my twin and told her we was on our way I made sure that the work went to the lab I really didn't want this nigga to get the same treatment as Noah I wanted this asshole to be dead as soon as the lid get closed I didn't want him to breath another breath, my twin wasn't picking up her phone I just hopped nobody told her about the plane but it was only a few knew about it and Bang was with me, Blaze was going to do the same shit so if she did know Bags would be the mouth work.

We got to Brownsville and my palms was sweaty I've been waiting to put my mark on this nigga life since his name came to my knowledge I got to Union Ave when my phone began ringing when I answered it was Nora.

"Where are you?" she asked.

"Pulling up now"

"No don't go to the church they're watching it I don't know how but he's been found. Go over to dead man hill we're over there."

I called Bang and told him where to go; but this shit wasn't sounding right. How the fuck did they know about him when nobody but family knew where we buried the nigga I just hoped we didn't have a Bull on our team, I drove pass the church and seen the caution tape going around the shell of the church and as I drove I also noticed two undercover cop cars I double parked and got out, I didn't want to make it look like I knew anything about so I just walked the one way block Blaze stayed in his car I just wanted to see what they knew or was anybody talking about it, my phone started ringing and of course it was Nora.

"Where the fuck is you?"

"I'm around the church checking.."

"Get the fuck off that block and get over here. We're in the tennis part and hurry up."

I jumped back I my car and just pulled off I called Bang and told him where to go.

Once I reached the place where she wanted to meet I noticed her car along with a few of our peoples cars also, when I got out Tap came over to me and filled me in on what was going on while I was gone, she also let me know my sister knew but really didn't know about Mike when we got inside the little area and what I was seeing was like a scene in a mob movie, it wasn't that much light out they had Sonny tied to the nets naked while kneeling on some broken glass and rocks he looked like he was in a fight with a professional boxer with his face all beaten and bloody he looked up he couldn't barely fully open his eyes but when he seen who just joined the party he knew his life was over, I walked over to where they had him my wife was behind the ball machine but it wasn't for tennis it was for baseball I walked over to him and asked

"Why have you come to me? Why did you kill my son?" when he didn't answer I went to turn up the pressure on the machine than I asked again but this time I was behind the thing. "Why you come to my spot?" he didn't answer at first than I shot a baseball at his chest "Tell me what I want to know" my twin came to me and said

"Let's get this over with I need to find out what happened to Mike" while we was talking Sonny said something but I didn't hear it I looked and asked.

"What was that?"

"My uncle sent me, he said whoever was there they die"

"Who's your uncle?" when he answered that I didn't want to believe him.

"My uncle Denny but everybody call him Blue. He sent me" my heart begun pounding, I than asked myself. How did he know that name? I could've understood just knowing the name Blue but he knew his full name I went and untied him I gave him that you're safe but also dead look and said.

"Thank you very much but you're still going to die, you have too"

"Look I'll do whatever you want.." I walked away from him and told my people to kill him and leave him there. My wife, twin, Bang and I walked out the park to our cars and I pulled my twin aside.

"What boy?" she asked looking at me like I was stupid from what I've just done.

"What do you know about this dude Mike?"

"Why?" she shot back.

"I don't think he's your type"

I didn't tell her what I done, well not yet exactly we all got in our cars my wife got in my car with me and pulled off I don't know where that nigga fell but what I do know is he won't be coming back I had my music on and was listening to an old M.O.P classic, now that that part of my life was over I had to get to this money we was all on our way to check on our product, my twin called when I answered she said something I didn't but also was a little okay with.

"Talk to me sis"

"On this ride I don't need you. Take your wife home and focus on her we got this."

"Alright call if you need me" I looked at my wife and asked

"What you want to get into?"

"It's late I'm pregnant and I'm ready to get in the tub and go to bed" when she said that I asked playfully

"What, I can't get no loving tonight

"Boy please, we just finished this nigga you just gotten back to the city I'm tired let's go home"

As I drove these old streets of mines I couldn't help but to think damn these used to be my streets now I own half this city and I was sure that motherfuckers wanted us out the picture but with my strength and my twin brain it wasn't going to happen, as I drove I seen something that had has gotten me upset there was a few police with their guns drawn at a family in a car I looked at my wife and stopped the car.

"Babe don't get out of this car" she said

"If I don't then they kill that family or the dad and who's to say that they won't try that with me? This is my city and these motherfuckers ain't getting away with another murder" after saying that I stepped out of my car with my gun drawn I told my wife to call Nora and let her know there were a few people out with their phones shit I hated seeing I shot in the air once I've had they attention that's when everybody else got out with their guns.

"Now that I have your attention you all are going to let them go with no problems or as you can see you all will be heading to the morgue one was about to move until a shot at his feet stopped him, one of the officers came to me, guess he was over the bullshit and said.

"Why don't you and your people get back.."

"Not until you and yours do the same." The look in his eyes told me his next move so I stopped that thought I aimed my gun at his face and said.

"If you really think this won't happen than you're crazier than you look. You see you niggaz do whatever you feel but not tonight. You see you don't get it this is my shit now get in your cars or you just won't make it home trust me."

We was in a standoff for a few minutes that's when they all got in their cars and pulled off the driver got out and came and thanked me I just told her and her family to go home then we all got in our rides than we all left. I was thinking about what I have and what I could be losing but this was me from the beginning to the end this was me it was late out and we was on our way to see the work we have just gotten although I already knew it was on point, my phone started buzzing and my wife answered she put it on speaker and my twin said in a voice that showed me she was pissed.

"I want you to go home. That shit was fucking stupid. Go fucking home I'll call you in the morning" after my wife hung up I went towards the Bronx while everybody else went to work, Kiss was quiet the whole drive home, she hadn't said one word.

I pulled into my driveway and before I could even stop the car my baby tried to jump out I pressed hard on the brakes and she got out, I really hated when she gets like this with the one answered questions and the lame hi and by's I sat in my car for a few more minutes than I got out when I stepped inside my wife was waiting at the door with fire on her eyes.

"Are you the dumbest motherfucker out here or what? The cop's babe, now I know that you're.." before she could've finished what she was going to say my phone started ringing.

"Yes twin" I answered in a tired on verge of getting upset voice.

"I'm coming to your house" after she said that the phone went dead, my wife and I stood there for a few minutes than I had to break the tension.

"I'm sorry babe"

"I can't lose you right now boy so slow your Hercules down just a little"

We was in the family room talking about what's next when my doorbell had rung, I went to get it leaving my wife laying on the sofa. When I opened the door Blaze, Bang, Yani, and twin was standing there.

"Get inside, we need to talk" Nora said pushing pass me.

We was all in the family room my wife was at the bar making drinks, my twin started talking without looking my way she said.

"I need you to sit down for a little. No matter of fact I need you to find out what happened to Mike" that was an easy job I thought to myself. "You put all of our hard work and freedom on the line for what. Somebody you don't even know? That was a dumb move you done earlier" than she stood up taking a sip of her Long Island Iced Tea "Don't always go in head first. And please boy don't play with my life. I want you to get some people together so you can find Mike good night"

Once they were gone I went in my studies and begun writing a poem my wife walked in with a drink and a blunt I doubted if she knew what was bothering me I was just glad she was there, I was quiet while she asked the unanswered relationship question

"Are you okay babe?"

"Yeah just got something on my mind"

"What?" she asked

"I had done something that would make my sister probably hate me"

"Which is?"

"Killed Mike"

I told her everything that happened who he was what he done our conversation had to had went on for maybe forty-five minutes than we both took a little rest.

Chapter 22

Nora

I couldn't sleep when I got home I went in my den and turned on my music and my T.V I was channel surfing when I seen a news reporter was saying.

"We have an I.D on the body that dropped out the sky but due to family request we will not be leaking his information but what I can say is that it was one of our own a decelerated officer of the law and we all are praying for the family of this officer."

I was relieved when I heard that so it couldn't of have been Mike that they've been talking about; but I do know that something has happened cause he hasn't answered none of my calls or returned any. I couldn't bury another guy and it wasn't like I even loved him just the fact that he was mine.

It was 8 in the morning when I noticed that my phone was blinking it was my twin he called me ten times, What the hell was this about? I called him back sounding tired.

"What the fuck is wrong with you ass? Why were you calling me like that?"

"We need to talk" he sounded serious that's when I got up a little more

"What's wrong you sound serious? Did something happen?"

"Just meet me at the Lounge"

"Okay" was all I said than we hung up.

I went to take a nice hot shower and thought about how twin sounded on the phone and since when have he ever needed to see me this early? I stood under the hot waterfalls soaping up my lovely body, I took me a fifteen minute shower then I stepped out of the marble stand in shower, I covered up in my Louis Vuitton towel and went to get dressed I didn't need to over dress so I just picked out a simple two-piece O-Looche pants suit I put on my O-looche open toe and heel ankle boots, I didn't feel like doing my hair so I threw on my curly short cut lace front wig on than I left, while leaving I threw on my O-Looche trench coat I called my twin and told him I was coming to meet with him I also called Blaze and Bang. Yani and Boe was taking care of the business I didn't know what James needed to talk about so early and why was he sounding so distance once I was done dressing I left my house I wasn't going to put in any work so I left my guns when I opened my garage going for my car I noticed a car that never been in this area parked across the street from me, I didn't pay too much attention just got in my car than pulled off, while driving I called my twin and told him that I was on my way I didn't know what was bothering him but I needed him to be on point while he's looking for Mike.

I remember the first time we met, Mike and myself at an art gallery when I seen Mike he was looking at some ugly but real expensive art work I was with Yani we was supposed to had meet up with some chic that felt that her feet got stepped on. I didn't know why but out of everything in this place the only art I wanted to see was Mike he was basically the sexiest man in the place he was dressed in a grey and black Donnetti sharkskin set and matching boxed front hard bottoms as soon as I laid my eyes on him I needed to see who he was his milk chocolate complexion his juicy plumped lips type that you could just suck through that right kiss, his sharp sexy eyes I was with Yani when I had walked over to where he stood and he had the little air around him smelling so good, I was also looking like me I had on my red and black Emporio Armani Plunge neck velvet gown on with matching red bottoms I had my own hair in that day and I had my girl Babs come over to hook me up, he looked up and noticed me than came over looking like fine art himself. When he reached over to where I stood it felt like shock wave was running through my thongs, he spoke spitting his little game but I really wasn't paying attention to his words.

Mike and I became a couple although his little business wasn't doing that well I gave him a shot and what a shot he made it out to be, Mike done all that he could've done to keep a smile on my face, now I don't know where the fuck he's at. I reached the Lounge and seen my twins car along with Blaze and Bangs ride, it was a rainy day out and this man wants to meet me when he suppose to be trying to figure out what happened to Mike.

When I walked inside the Lounge I noticed all the boys talking when they looked my way they stopped their conversation I looked at them and said jokingly.

"What's this, a hostile takeover? I'm ready to go out for mines" my twin looked and said with a serious look.

"Nora sit we need to talk. But first let's get a drink. Long Island Iced Tea? Am I right?" I really didn't like the movements that was going on

"James please can you stop moving? You're making me nervous, sit down and talk" I said pulling out a seat for me.

"What do you always say about your money and freedom? Don't fuck with it. Well the saying goes for you as well" he said bringing me my drink.

"Boy what the fuck are you talking about?" I asked close to getting highly upset I looked at Blaze and asked "What the hell is going on?"

"I just went to Miami and I went with company and one of the people that came isn't here and won't be anymore." I didn't like what he was saying I took a sip of my drink and got into boss mode.

"Whatever, I told you to take care of something and I want all of you on your post right now" as I was leaving I looked back at my twin with the most disappointed look and said "Find out what happened to Mike" what was said next stopped me from moving.

"Mike's dead twin, I killed him" not that did he just say that but what he said next was even more insane "He was Police twin" I turned around and when I seen the look in his eyes it told me he believed his bullshit.

"What the fuck are you saying?" I asked.

"You made a mistake don't worry about.." I couldn't listen to this anymore.

"What the.. Are you listening to yourself? I was fucking a cop?" I didn't want to hear the shit no more so I was out the door when he said.

"The cat they talking about on the News,, that's Oh-boy" he said this displaying a police badge I didn't want to look at it cause I can see he wasn't lying "I seen him and Bags talking one day then Bags confirmed it at the party"

I went to my office and James followed, all I could think about was how much shit was this motherfucker was getting on us, we reached the office and James closed the door behind us, I went to my bar and fixed me a drink then went and sat behind my desk.

"How long was that relation going on for?" James asked.

"I don't know 9 maybe ten months on the low. Why you ask?"

"Did you take him anywhere or shown him anything important?" I had to think about everything he knew and who was his so-called friends he introduced me too.

"Not nowhere important" than I thought about it "This shit's going to get ugly"

"Don't worry about it I got it; besides this was my doing" he said taking a puff of his blunt.

"Hell no we're going to ride this shit together. Cause if he had people behind him than they're about to come, and we're going to need everybody"

"And everything" James finished what I was going to say I took out my phone and called Blaze and told him and Bang to come up, while we waited James and I tried to recall all the faces and names Mike showed me over the past few months.

Bang and Blaze came in smoking a blunt Bang passed it my way I hadn't smoked I was too upset to do anything, we sat there trying to figure out our next move, I dint know who his partner was I called Vasquez and filled him in on what I needed from him being that he was inside the doors.

James, Blaze, and Blunt was sitting down talking Blaze told my twin of all the places that I've taken Mike too. I couldn't face being the reason of everybody losing their freedom and I'm always the one reminding them on my freedom and money. My head was killing me I got up to leave then my phone started ringing I answered it Vasquez and he said to me.

"It's a manhunt on whoever done it"

"Do they have any leads?" I asked

"No not that I know of." he responded.

"Okay just keep me posted"

"No problem"

Once we hung up I went to let them know what was told to me.

"Good now let's continue getting this money" James said I looked at James and said

"No.. I still need you out of sight for a while. That shit is still out there"

Blunt and I left the office leaving the rest of them still there I couldn't believe it that I slipped up like that I told Blunt that I needed to be alone and he took me to the one place where I can find piece, with my money.

Chapter 23

Narrator

The precinct was busy, but unlike any other day on this particular one the cop's are about to hear the news they was waiting to hear since the day the heinous act happened, the niece of the mysterious man that's been discovered has decided to walk in the precinct and say what she knew about that day, she stayed at her uncle's house and he shared a lot of important things with the young nineteen year old and knowing what she knew she was shaken of the thought in going through with this, standing at the desk nervous and afraid the girl waited to be seen and when she has been it was by Vasquez, when her uncle told her about the twins and his case he told his niece if he was to never come back go to an officer Davenport, Vasquez walked over to the young lady and said with a smile.

"Hello how can I help you?"

"Yes I'm looking for officer Davenport I want to give some information about a crime"

"Whoa you said a crime happened? And where was this?"

"It's about my uncle he went with someone and I would like to talk to officer Davenport"

"Okay I'll go for officer Davenport. Can I ask. Where have this crime taken place?"

"I don't know it's all over the news"

"What are you saying that..."

"Yes the cop that you all found is my uncle now can you please go get officer Davenport!!"

When those words was said everything came to a stop once that happened Vasquez took the young lady to an investigation room and went to get the officer before going there he slid in the exit and made a call the phone rang three times

"Hello"

"Get over to my job now" he said to the person he called.

While driving to her quiet place, Nora received a call she than told Blunt to stop the car.

"Get to Vasquez job right now" was all Nora said

Going to the 49th precinct Nora called James to let him know where she's going and where to meet her, she was getting nervous Vasquez told her who had walked in the precinct and what she was saying Nora told Blunt to hurry up and get to the Bronx, Nora was locked in get that bitch mode she was thinking that everything she has accomplished for herself and her family and she wasn't going to allow anybody to come in the way her any of their freedom.

Getting to the Bronx was a quick drive, her twin was already here by the time she and Blunt arrived she noticed his and Bags cars parked across the street from the precinct Nora didn't feel like wasting any time on this job so without hesitating she got out that's when everybody else done the same they seen a lot of pedestrians walking the street Nora looked at her twin and said

"Look stay in your car, I don't need you to be recognized"

"So why did you tell me to come over here?"

"Just in case"

Nora, Bags, and Blunt walked in the precinct, not knowing to any of the police that the individuals that they're looking for has just walked into their doors, Nora walked over to the desk and asked to see officer Vasquez.

Sitting in the cold room as she waited for officer Davenport all the worst things she could think about happening to her if word got out that she mentioned their names was coming to mind.

The girl was sitting in the interrogating room for about ten minutes she remembered the first time her uncle brought her to his job and how much fun she had with him she begun to cry the more she thought about him. Yes she thought she had to say something just as that thought came to her mind the door opened and officer Vasquez walked in she was a little at eased when she seen him walk in but she wasn't ready for the next face that she seen Nora walked in like she owned the place she gave the young girl one of the iciest looks she has ever seen, the young girl heart begun rapidly pounding she looked like her life was about to be stopped at that very second.

"Please have a seat" Nora said "We don't have that much time so please,, sit." The girl sat down and Nora begun "look I'm not here to scare you or nothing in a sort, but if you decide to speak that pretty brownstone duplex out there on 127th owned by Mrs. Linda and Mr. Albert Brown you see he told me about you but what he didn't know was that I have people who can find the real you" Nora stood up and said fixing her clothes. "Like I said I'm not here to scare you or hurt you I'm here to enlighten you. Have a good day Lisa"

Nora and her guys walked out just as fast as they walked in. Outside they each has gotten to their cars without another second wasted they all pulled off.

Inside the precinct Vasquez went to the interrogating room where Lisa was still placed she looked at him in disbelief and asked.

"Do you feel proud of yourself cop"

"Little girl shut the fuck up and listen. She's giving you a way out keep your mouth shut look I told Davenport that you're here he's on his way" Vasquez said before leaving the room "Think about you parents unless you want them dead. It's up to you" seconds later after Vasquez left her vision a male officer walked in holding two steaming cups and a woman officer walked in.

"Hello I'm Officer Kenneth Davenport and you are?" Lisa looked at the officer and just got up and left, Davenport looked at his partner and said jokingly "Damn I looked that bad"

"Just today" his partner responded with a smile.

Davenport went back to his office to get back to figuring out who killed his partner he knew of the case he was working on but what he didn't know but did think he knew who done it there was everything that his partner put together on the twins on his desk, Davenport was one of the streets toughest cops when he had a feeling in his gut than that's exactly what it was and he would never stop until his thought was proven.

Nora was in the back seat on the phone talking some business while Blunt drove her through the streets of New York she heard of some old guy name John trying to open up on one of her areas in Harlem usually she'll send Bang or Boe but she wanted to see the guy so she told Blunt where to go

"I want you to take me to 127th and Saint Nick there's somebody out there I want to see"

At first Blunt kept quiet and just drove Nora to her destination than he asked.

"This dude you're going to see is who?"

"Somebody who is fucking up in my City"

"Don't tell me this is that old dude, How far can he make it?" Blunt had asked than Nora said something he has never heard.

"No matter what age a person is when they start if their product whatever it is if it's tight than people could be going to his show. Besides he's living in my City and not paying rent not a great start"

They reached their destination and just like it was said this John dude was in his gate dressed like he was ready for bed Nora looked and laughed at what she was looking at, stepping out of the car Nora seen a little how he was doing his shit which wasn't too out there like a lot of niggaz she know even some of hers approaching the gate she looked John in his eyes and just walked in his gate.

"I think you and I need to have a discussion" Nora said

"First of all what the fuck is in your panties for you to think you can walk in my shit like that?"

"You're telling me you're in my City and you don't know who the landlord is? Okay let me tell you this."

"Let's stop all this testosterone shit and you tell me why are we having this conversation" as they stood there talking some addicts was coming and each time they came they has gotten turned away Nora looked at John and said

"I can make it easy for you or real hard your call"

"Look whoever you are you're fucking with my money and trust me you don't want to do that" John said with fire in his eyes

"Finally we have a common ground. Look my first intentions were to come and see if we can find an understanding but I see that's not going to happen. So here's what's going to happen if I hear that you sold one piece of rock white sand bud whatever you have that will be your invitation to your own funeral" John looked in the eyes of this woman and seen this wasn't an idle threat once the woman and her goon had left John got on his cell and made a call he was hoping that he would never had to make

"Talk"

"We have to go to work"

"When and who?" was all that was asked from the other side

"Some bitch that think she owns this City"

"If you're talking of who I think you are than dawg she do. And that's a situation you don't want" John didn't care about who the bitch was if it was Trump he wouldn't care it was time to see somebody insides he went inside where his family was he looked at his wife and kids and thought if he couldn't feed them than what, he knew that if shit was to hit the fan than this City has to get smelly but if his arm don't want to move with him than what was his next move. Every since he and his people ever had to go to work he never had gotten a response like that, John never ran away from anything in his life and at the age he was he wasn't going to start he even had to go to work against the law and haven't ran so who the fuck was this chick, his daughter came and asked him a question but he was so into his thoughts he hadn't heard what was said. He called his boy back to find out who this chick was but this time the phone just ranged his wife came in the room where he was and done something he really didn't need her doing

"Your kids are hungry" upset of the earlier events he tried to ignore her but unlike any other female you try to ignore she done and kept on going than she said something that made John respond

"Maybe I should go find Derrick so he can feed us and than give me something else. What you think?" John stood up and calmly walked over to where she stood and said

"Go ahead do it, he already think you're nothing but a fuck so go ahead go suck some dick. Your lazy ass need to bring some money in this place anyway."

"You ain't shit just like your no shit parents" John parents had been murdered on his 13th birthday in front of him since that day he became something fucked up, he grabbed her by the neck and quickly let her go he said quietly.

"Please get out of this room, go do what you feel but please get away from me right now" his wife was tough but there was times when that tough shit didn't work and right now was one of those times.

Lisa was in the train going nowhere with no money thinking about her uncle and her killers and that they won't be paying for what they've done and she began crying she felt alone now that her uncle was gone she didn't have nobody. Unaware of her surroundings there was someone in the train following her move as she cried some of the passengers tried helping that's when he made his way over to her extending his hand

"Hello sweetie can I give you a hand or shoulder you can cry on?" Bags said to the girl, she looked up and smile not knowing who he was she was taken aback from what seen standing in front of her, she just smirked and said "No" Bags just went and sat down and remained following her.

She stayed on the train until it reached the Bronx and got off Fordham.

Bags was still sitting on the train when Lisa gotten off he done the same not paying attention she went straight to some guy and he begun embracing her, Bags kept his eyes on the pair than took out his phone and took some shots of the couple Bags than called his boss

"Do you see her?" Nora asked

"Yes and I guess her little boyfriend, I have a few shots of them on my phone"

"Good, where are you?"

"Bronx Fordham road"

"Okay stay on her I want to know where she's going?"

He was in his office looking at the case and thought to himself "Damn Mike you had to do all the hard shit" and then he started wondering Why the hell his niece asked to see me but run when he get there, one thing about Davenport was he knew how to read and he knew that girl wanted to talk to him and the one officer who had some contact with her was Vasquez, leaving the interrogation room davenport went to the direction of Vasquez desk but once there Vasquez wasn't there Davenport was a man that went by his gut feeling first this girl was screaming to see me than speaks to Vasquez than she runs away something didn't feel right with him and he was going to figure it out as soon as Davenport was about to leave he seen Vasquez walking towards his desk, unaware of his reasons of being at his desk Vasquez looked somewhat pleased to see Davenport.

"Hey brother, what's the visit for?" Vasquez asked

"We need to have a quick word, if you're not too you know"

"Um sure I'm getting off in a sec. Why don't we go get a drink? My treat" Vasquez said jokingly

"Sure thing brother" Davenport responded with caution in his eyes the two men went back to what it was they both was doing.

Back in his office Davenport went back to trying to figure out Mikes case, he was reading a page when he noticed a small paper with writing on it he picked it up and begun reading

"Going to Miami with James something weird about this I don't understand." James, Davenport had thought to himself who is this James? All he knew about was Nora and her team this James he hadn't heard he knew that Nora was a twin but not to a guy, he kept going over the case tying to see what have Mike noticed. As he was still going over the work there was a knock on his door when he looked up there was Vasquez standing there.

"Ready for that drink buddy?" Vasquez asked

"Sure just let me put this up"

Once he was done in his office Davenport went to change so he can get in Vasquez head, he had a feeling he knew more than what he's been saying. Davenport has gotten ready to leave when he walked out of the precinct Vasquez was on his new motorcycle waiting.

"Where are we going?" Davenport asked

"We're going to a nice bar my people own"

Chapter 24

James

Putting all the work I had to put in over the years or in my life I've never had to put a cop to sleep, and although he was a cop he was also my twin man and I hope my sister don't hate me for the decision I made, shit I rather she be mad at me instead of us talking to one another behind glass, I was on my way to go see what's going on with my mother since we been shutting this city down I really haven't been around her so I called and told her I was on my way but she didn't pick up so I just left a I love you message not so long ago I wasn't able to write or call shit I didn't know she was alive now I'm able to tell her that I love her.

I reached Brooklyn at around 3 in the afternoon and took that long drive to my mother's house. As I drove to through my neighborhood looking at what was out here was crazy but I had to laugh because I knew they had caught a taste of the Sting.

When I reached Crown Heights it was around 4:15 in the afternoon. I went to the grocery around my mom's way and picked up some of my favorites so I could have that good mama's food, Steak, Idaho potatoes, fresh cut green beans, and all the toppings, for her mother's family gravy, her butter bisques, I went to pay and just like every time she sees me she threw on her gorgeous smile.

"I haven't seen you in a while"

"A man like me can't be placed in one area for too long" after I paid she said

"You do know that you don't have to pay for everything. You can get some things for free" she said with a smile.

"If I was young love I might've would take you on those words but in this time of my life I'm not that guy. My wife has my heart" I said while paying for the food.

As I left the grocery when I walked out a female officer was at my car giving me a ticket, at first I was going to sweet talk her but decided against it I just got in my car and continued what I was doing, I called my twin and informed her of my whereabouts she told me she's on her way.

I reached my mother's house after parking I got out grabbing the bags from the back seat I went to my mother's door I had the keys but the door wasn't locked, I walked in and dropped the bags when I walked inside when I seen what I saw, I heard talking and it looked like someone was trying to either rob or frighten my mother while the talking continued I took my gun out and cocked it back and walked in the room where the talking was coming from when I walked in there was at least five guys each had guns out, my mother's nurse was on the floor not moving face bloody and not paying attention one asked my mother.

"Where the fuck did they go? Lady trust me this isn't a game you.." I walked in without any question I said a small prayer and shot the closest to the door, once he dropped they was distracted that's when the one by the window got a shot in his head. I quickly went over to my mother's side aiming my gun at his face he seen the look in my eyes I was in killer mode.

"I'm right here, you step in my mother's home and disrespects her children knowing who the fuck we are, you want to see us I'm right here and believe me my twin is on her way." I looked at my mother kissed her on the cheek and sent her to her room. And said to him

"I done seen a lot of stupid motherfucker's but you" I said shooting another one of his boys than aiming my gun back at him.

"I wish you would. Sit your ass down" just as I said that I heard my twin's voice.

"What the fuck is this?"

"Come in here twin" I yelled out to her. She, Bang, and Boe came in all with guns out I seen the look in his eyes he knew he was dead I looked at my twin and said.

"These young men came over to have a word with us but the thing is mommies nurse isn't breathing and this young man right here was holding his gun" my twin came and sat beside me and said.

"Yes sir I'm here. You wanted to see me?"

Chapter 25

Nora

Once we left the precinct we was on our way to one of my laboratories in Brooklyn, East New York I couldn't believe that we might have to go to war with the fucking N.Y.P.D these was my streets and it wasn't nobody was going to take them from me and that's exactly what that motherfucker was trying so no I wasn't mad at him cause I would've done the same. All of a sudden I started thinking about my mother I might just go see her when I'm done.

We reached Brooklyn looking at how these streets changed made me mad but then again I was also good because my stamp was out here there was a few cop cars zooming pass and I had thought that this wasn't the time for any of us to go to war especially not with the cops I just hoped Bags was still on her ass. We got to E.N.Y and drove to New Lots it was like the president was out here the way we was driving through the borough and every spot we went through eyes was on us, riding through this neighborhood always brings me back to when I met Blunt and all the shit that we had accomplished while I drove my cell went off when I looked to see who it was I seen my twins name.

"Speak" I said to him

"I'm going to see mom"

"Okay I'll be over, just have to take care of something. Tell mom I said hi"

Bangs car was beside mine, I called him and told him of our new plans I called Blaze

"Yeah boss"

"Look I'm going to make a little stop, so I want you to take care of this okay"

Once we hung up Bang, myself, and Boe drove off to my mother's Yani and Blaze stayed back to take care of work, I haven't been spending time with my mom's but I made sure that she was taken care of.

Driving though this New York compared to the old New York the feeling was different money was better work was more potent (well my work is potent) shit even the competition was better, but it was a little funny how the bitches was behind their men back then, but now the man is this bitch who is the boss.

My twin was over at my mother's house waiting on us, although I was a little upset at him I couldn't be mad because if he wouldn't of have done it I would've (once I would've found out) We owned everything that's been moving and if we didn't we had money coming from it I had everything I ever wanted but as I drove watching these people while they walked I noticed one thing that these people had that I don't and that was a child, but as soon as it came to mind it left.

We reached my mother's neighborhood and I noticed my twins car parked in front of my mother's house so I got out of my own then we went to my mother's house which was opened a little when I stepped inside what I seen was crazy it looked like she had just gotten robbed the only thing I could've said was.

"What the fuck is this?" than I heard my twin yelled from the family room

"Come in here twin" Bang, myself, and Boe took out our guns and when we walked in the room what I seen was great, there were three bodies on the floor and when I noticed my mother's nurse my mode just changed my twin was sitting at the table with some guy with his gun aimed at him there was also two other guys there looking like they wanted to take a shit on themselves I went and sat next to my twin and he said looking at the guy that none of us knew.

"These young men came to have a word with us but the thing that I can't understand is why the fuck was they holding a gun to mommy not to mention her nurse." he said gesturing towards her dead body I looked at the guy and said.

"Yes sir I'm here. You wanted to see me? Look I know that you're not that dumb to just come at us on your own, so I want you to think about tomorrow"

"And what's tomorrow?" he asked frighteningly.

"A day you should want to see it?" I asked, I looked at Bang and said "I want you to take my mother to my house, It's about to get real noisy" my twin looked and said.

"I'm not going to be asking you the same question a hundred times I'm going to asks once tell me or not I'll find out. Who the fuck sent you?" his boy seemed like he was going to move and Boe made him think differently I seen in his eyes that he wanted to say something but was scared too

"I don't think that you have loved ones cause death is right here and you're thinking about" before I could've finished what I was saying James shot him in the face looked at his boy and told him to sit, once he did James said.

"You heard the question that was asked" than he looked at the lifeless dumbass on the floor.

"None of us knew her she had your people followed to get to you. She was talking about some guy name Noah other than that I don't know"

"So you come to kill without knowing why or who you're supposed to kill. You're a fool and.." I didn't let him finish like he done to me I shot the guy in the face, the one that Boe knocked out was still on the floor James went to get him up, once he was able to listen and understand we sat him down in front of us.

"What we're going to do is let you breath so you could go tell the bitch we're coming for her" I called my girl Amanda and gave her the names I needed her to do background checkups on than I hung up.

Once we left the house we locked the door than called our cleaners, I left the keys in the mailbox than we got in our cars then we all pulled off. We let the guy go I told Boe to follow him; we all went our own way my twin was going home being that Kiss was close to giving birth. Damn that nigga Noah is still fucking around even from the dirt, it's been month's since he murdered my girl Mells and I miss my sis but being that his sister wife mother or whoever the bitch is miss him so much than fuck it I'm just going to have to bring them together.

I had a feeling that somebody was going to bring that bitch back from the grave but I just thought it would've been a cop; don't get me wrong none of us was worried but instead of worrying about the N.Y.P.D now we have this dumbass family trying to get some payback which they'll see that their check will bounce, this was something I really don't need to happen not only for me but everybody that rode behind me, I went home to check up on my mother I know she was shaken up by what she seen she loved Brittney she was the best nurse my mother have had in a while and to see her final seconds on this earth in that way,, damn.

When I got to Connecticut I hurried to my home and when I got there I seen Bangs car in my driveway I parked behind his and quickly hopped out and went inside I knew m mother would be safe here since I have gotten security since that last incident I didn't like it but it's better to be safe walking around than getting fucked up by them nasty ass maggots when I walked in my home I heard my mother and Bang talking in the families room I heard my mother talking with a broken heart about her nurse I embraced my mother while she cried on my shoulders my mother looked at me and said.

"Why have they done that to her she was just a kid" I didn't need my mother crying about this so I said'

"Ma let me and Brian have a conversation about what happened today okay" I told my help to take her to the guest room, than I said to Bang. "This shit is getting crazy Bang. They went to my mother's door and this nigga been dead for months; what the fuck!!" I said knocking over some glass figurines, "Not to mention if these motherfuckers figure out who done that to Mike we going to need more power, and we're also going to have to find out about this nigga family I want you to find out who the fuck his aunt is" I needed all this situation bullshit off our backs, I had a lot of missed calls and messages from Vasquez I didn't checked them just kept talking to Bang, I knew whatever I needed done he could get it done within the right timing while we talked one of my helps came in with a frightened look on her face.

"What is it?" I asked

"It's your mot..the.. It's your mother ma'am" when she said that I didn't like the look that was in her eyes

"What the fuck is going on?" what she said next had fucked my head up,

"Your mother, she isn't breathing" when she said those words my mind just went blank I didn't want to believe that she had said what was said, I got up and went to go check on my mother I didn't want to go to the room and see what was behind the door, and when I did my mother was laying on the bed looking like she had no worries I told Bang to call my bother while I called the ambulance.

"Hello how may"

"Fuck all that, my mother's not breathing" I said cutting her off I told them my address than hung up I went to see if my mother was still breathing but couldn't, my phone begun ringing when I seen who was calling it was my twin.

"What the fuck is going on over there?!" he asked

"Just come over" is all I said

Chapter 26

Narrator

Vasquez and Davenport sat in the far corner of the fancy bar and spoke on what they expected to had happen to Officer Mike but little did Vasquez know he was the one who was being studied, while Davenport shot question after question to Vasquez trying to see anything that said that he knew of what is really going on but as they spoke to Davenport he could see nothing, the two police sat in the establishment having drinks one after the next.

The time was getting late and the two fellow officers was now falling over they kicking themselves falling down, security walked over to the two men Davenport the most drunk of the two begun making a scene, Vasquez escorted his friend out now that he now had Davenport incoherent he took that as a sign to figure what Davenport knew on the twins well more James and the case and if there was anything leading to him Vasquez held Davenport up while he tried to get all the information he could get out of him, Vasquez asked Davenport

"So buddy, tell me what's new with the Officer Lewis case?"

"Well there's not that much, except this note saying who he was with the day he went missing" Davenport responded

"Is there anyone in particular?" Vasquez asked

"I got my eyes on somebody. What do you have on the case? Davenport asked in a drunken stupor

"Not as much as you pal" Vasquez had to think fast knowing that he had to get to Davenports office, he tried to stop a cab, it took five minutes for one to stop an Uber had stopped when Vasquez placed Davenport in the backseat took out a wad of money peeled off five crispy hundred dollar bills and said to the Spanish female driver.

"My friend here is a cop I want you to drive him around."

"I can't do that" the driver said; but when she seen what he had in his hand she begun coming to her senses.

"Take this" he said giving her the money than he gave her an extra hundred dollar bill. "When he sober up take him wherever he need to go"

Once Vasquez was alone he rushed over to his car and jumped in he had to get back to work and get to Davenports office but knowing that wouldn't be an easy thing to do so he called in one of the women officers that he knew would be there he called in a favor, being that he had some dirt on her he knew that she wouldn't say no, her phone rung about three times until Vasquez heard her Latin voice.

"Yes Vasquez"

"I really need you" with the sweat running down the side of his now red cheek and it wasn't from the drinks he haven't touched, he knew if Davenport was to find out everything and body linked to the twins his life as he knew it would be over, he said to Ruiz "I need you to get to Davenport office and pick up something on his desk"

Always following his gut Davenport had placed a bug on Vasquez calling in a favor Davenport had help from the F.B.I listening on this call while Vasquez told Ruiz what to look for the Feds was getting all the information they needed to get for their warrant. Davenport was sitting in his living room with the other officers along with the hidden camera in Davenport's office they all watched in disbelief while Officer Ruiz rummaged through all of his paper work.

The Sergeant over the surveillance was walking around looking over everything that they've managed to put together, Davenport stood in the corner of the room puffing on a cigarette the Sergeant walked over to where he stood with a smile he said to Davenport.

"You did well Officer Davenport, we will get to this immediately"

"I'm not worried about this. My partner was murdered that's what I'm trying to figure out"

"Like I said Davenport, We'll get to it"

Lisa laid on her boyfriends bed with her small perky breast exposed close to tears while her boyfriend was under the covers head between her thighs, upset of earlier events she stopped him and begun crying. Lost by her actions the young man went in and tried to kiss only to get pushed away.

"What the fuck babe. What's going on?" he asked.

"I'm sorry it's not you I'm just thinking about my uncle" she said crying.

"Yeah babe no doubt we don't have to"

"No you don't get it" she said looking down "I think I know who killed him"

"So tell the cop's than" he boyfriend just holding worrisome in his eyes for the young teen knowing how much trouble she's had endured her young life with her mother dying and her dad the young boy just hugged his beautiful young girlfriend he looked her in her eyes and said with care

"Go to the cop's babe this is hurting you, I'll be right there with you let's go" she stood up pushing him aside jumping off the bed although she liked what he was saying but she knew that if he was to get involved and try to help her they have girls that'll burry him.

"You don't know what you're talking about, these people are dangerous babe they'll.." Lisa's young protector stood up with his little manhood swinging between his legs he went to his girl and said to her not knowing who or what the fuck he was about to get involved with he went under his bed and took out his big brothers black 9mm he looked in the girls eyes knowing her fear but not listening to her words he said.

"Nobody is going to come fuck with us trust me I got you" feeling safe the young girl knew that if she would stay next to him any longer that's putting him in danger, she begun getting dressed while she got dressed Will begun doing the same.

"No,, don't" she said stopping him. "These people aren't your regular street niggaz these are some serious motherfucker's so please promise me that you won't follow me" Lisa gave William a kiss that he won't be able to forget than she left.

Outside Bags was sitting in his car waiting until he seen one of the two walk out the building he had been waiting in that spot for about an hour just as soon as a police was walking towards his car he seen the young woman walking out the building seeing this he started his engines instead of taking the train Lisa got in a cab (luckily his car has been dropped off,) he thought to himself. Bags followed Lisa's cab and called Nora but her phone just rung so he tried James and once again the phone just rung he said fuck it and just continued following the cab Bags remembered when James told him that he seen Mike and himself one time before and now that Mike's dead will Nora send James after him, was it enough that he informed them on Mikes intentions Bags thought Nora had saved Bags ass a few times in the past from Blaze but he didn't know who James was Bags stayed on the cab until he lost train of thought for a second that's when his car had crashed into another car causing him to flip his Range Rover over three times the other car which was a Ford Eco had a couple along with their two young daughters sitting in the backseat smashed against a parked car leaving them with minor injuries the driver had attended to his family than he went to check on the other driver but once he got to the scene it was hectic the car was totaled and the diver was automatically dead the young man turned back and went back to his family.

Lisa was in the cab on her way home thinking about her uncle and begun shedding tears, unaware of what just accrued behind her she decided not going home she told the driver.

"Instead of taking me home; can you take me to the 49th precinct please?"

"Sure thing" the driver shot back

Lisa knew what type of trouble she would be in if that lady was to find out she said something but her uncle was dead and she wanted his killer in jail, with her heart beating pass beats she took out her cell and called the number that her uncle gave her for emergencies she dialed the number three times but only gotten the answering machine she left texts VMs etc at this point she didn't care about what would happen all she wanted was to see them pay.

Once they've reached the 49th precinct and she gave the driver the last of what she had jumped out the cab doors and rushed through the doors and went straight for the reception desk.

"Yes deer how may I help you?" the old man asked, the young lady looked frightened but said.

"Yes I would like to see officer Davenport"

"Sorry Officer Davenport has been clocked out. Can I get you another Officer?" he asked

"Um no I'm really going to need Officer Davenport its urgent" she said

"Um sure thing; please have a seat"

It's been hours and Lisa was still waiting when her phone begun ringing

"Yes" she said quickly

"Yes I've gotten a few calls from this number. This is Eric Davenport. And I'm speaking with?"

"This is the niece of Officer Mike" when she said that it was an awkward silence.

"I have some valuable information that is very important to you" the line went quiet for a few seconds Lisa was about to hang up until she heard.

"I need you to wait there and I'll be on my way. And deer please don't talk to nobody I'll be there shortly"

Davenport was now sitting in his kitchen along with his wife sitting across from him speaking about his case and the one cop he thought was a good friend of his he finds out that he's on his radar, his wife has always been an open ear for her husband no matter what. Davenport asked his wife.

"If it was you what would you do? If your buddy…" his wife stopped him

"If it was me and I had a life, husband, two kids, etc. There's more than one other person on this planet"

The couple sat at the table and spoke which was feeling like forever until Davenport checked his phone listening to his voicemail once the person said who they was Davenport had quickly called, the two spoke and what was being said he couldn't believe it, he thought to himself All the investigating and all the hard work his partner Mike has put in on the case was finally about to pay off, he told the person he was talking to.

"I need you to wait there I'm on my way. And deer please don't talk to no one" Davenport quickly stood to his feet grabbing his gun and badge gave his wife a kiss and quickly ran out the door Davenport jumped in his car without another second wasted he pulled off Davenport was remembering a conversation him and his partner had about the two twins and the way they are but he didn't care about none of that, his partner was in the ground not to mention the people that his partner was trying to bring peace Davenport has went against the best of them but never no one like the twins but he wondered why was this the first time he's heard of the twins and from what he heard of about the two they should've been dead or even locked up and now their time is up Davenport casually thought to himself.

The accident was terrible the ambulance and police had the area blocked off and once they seen the driver they automatically knew he was dead after placing Bags in a body bag and all the spectators was glad about what they seen they all pulled off, there were police asking the driver about the details, after getting everything the family could've told they all went to the Hospital, now with Bags being in the coroners van there was no way to know what was going on which Nora and company will soon find out.

Reaching his place of work which was located in the Bronx Davenport was ready to put this case to rest Davenport parked his car than rushed through the doors of the 49th precinct, as soon as Davenport walked in and seen the young lady sitting there with a scared look on her face Davenport went and gotten a hot coffee and walked over to the young lady and said gingerly

"Would you like a cup of something hot?" when the young girl looked up and the look Davenport seen in her eyes he knew that he had to move quick after she took the semi hot cup Davenport led the girl to an empty interrogation room where he was now about to sit and help this young teen not knowing that all the information this girl was going about to give him was everything he needed to go after the twins, but was he really ready to go after them with knowing what he knew he thought to himself than looking at the young girl, niece of his partner the brother he took an oath for?

"Hell yeah" Davenport said to himself feeling a little bigger than regular walking pass his partner Mike's office he looked at the name that use to hold one of the best names he could've ever known "I'm ready" he said feeling he was close to bringing justice to all those he read about that the twins has done wrong too Davenport open the door to the only room he knew to himself that his always used

Chapter 27

Nora

Me, Blaze, and Blunt was in the waiting area of Bridgeport Hospital my mother was in the E.R James and Kiss hasn't shown due to her predicament I didn't want to believe that my mother was now dead nit when we just gotten back together, minutes later Boe, Yani and Bang had walked in and they all walked to where we stood Yani came over to me and said hugging onto me.

"How are you doing boss?" I nudged her off of me and said to everybody

"Look although we're here over a bad situation let's not lose any focus." I then looked at Blaze and asked "Did you hear from Bags?"

"Nah the last I spoke to him was at the precinct when you told him to follow that bitch" while we was speaking the Dr. quietly walked in holding a clipboard I was nervous from what would've been said, Bang, and Blaze had shut everything down like my mother was royalty making sure nobody else comes on this floor.

"Ms. Lee" he called my name I really didn't want to hear what was about to be said I took out my phone and called my twin I wasn't going to get this information without him, the phone had rung twice when I heard his voice.

"Wus sup twin. What they're saying about mommy?"

"I need you here with me. The doctor is right here now" I said knowing that he had other shit he was attending too. The doctor and I were talking for like three minutes when I heard my twin I thought to myself. How the fuck did he get here that fast? But fuck it he was here, I went to hug him I was confused I looked and he said

"I couldn't let you do this alone. I was on the highway already on my way when you called, but fuck that what's wrong with mommy?" he asked looking at the doctor which looked like he wanted to run home at that very moment.

"Like I was saying to Ms Lee, we have done all." I didn't hear nothing after the words your mother was gone, I glanced over to where James was and he had the doctor on the floor choking him while everybody was trying to get him off, when everything calmed down I went to go see my mother and when my twin had finally stopped being an animal he joined me.

We got to my mother's room while the nurse was placing the sheet over her head when I seen that I almost had blacked out.

"Stop" I yelled to her she looked afraid when she looked back. She left leaving me and my brother alone with her, my mother looked real peaceful we walked in the room and just stood there and looked at her while she rest. James said to me while still looking at my mom.

"You know with all that's happening and what's going to happen I think it'll be okay that she's going to chill with her son and her man. I know it sounds bad but look at it like this motherfuckers came to her home.. So yes it's going to be okay" listening to what he was saying at first sounded a little fucked up but when I had thought about it he was speaking the truth I looked at him and said.

"Okay let's close this fucking city down. But first I have to make a call."

Leaving my mother's room I told the nurse

"You better take care of her"

We all got outside and jumped in our car's I had a few messages from Bag's but I couldn't check them, I was going to my club to clear my head but no I wanted to end this shit,, and fast so I just called James phone

"Yo twin what's going on" he responded

"We're going to Uncle Dee. We're going to need more ammo. Not to mention we have to tell him about mommy"

"Look twin this is not only one family. This is a family and also the police. Did your girl do that background check on all those motherfucker's who ran up in mommy house?"

"Right as we speak. Don't worry your pretty black skin about shit we're good" after hanging up I called my uncle, I know that he would probably be sleeping being what time it was but I needed his help; the phone rang like four time then I heard a tired.

"This better be important lil girl"

"Yes it is. I'm coming to your house right now, and I have company" I hung up the phone and headed to my uncle house.

When we all reached my uncle house in Bayside Queens it was about two in the morning and I noticed my uncle waiting out front of his house with a drink in his hand. I didn't understand why my uncle had rather live out here in Forest Hills.

"You wasn't playing huh girl?" he said looking at the family.

"I'm sorry" I said with that sad baby girl look.

"Look my wife and son is sleep. Keep it quiet in m house"

We all walked in after my uncle and it looked different from the last time I was here, it looked a little too womanly, my uncle looked at me and James.

"You two come with me." Then he said to the rest "The rest of you I only talk once, this ain't near one of your place so disrespect my home I disrespect your lives"

My uncle, James, and I went to my uncles smoke room, to have some family time, we still haven't told him about my mother yet and really didn't want too but of course he asked that one question.

"So what's going on with the two of you?" he asked walking towards his desk I looked at my twin and never lying to my uncle I said.

"We have a problem"

"Which family?" he asked

"The N.Y.P.D" James responded, my uncle gave me that father look than James told him everything that just happened and when he said what happened to my mother I seen in his eyes that fucked him up he said to me.

"Remember what I told you about this life and families?" he asked me "I said that there're some families you can and can't fuck with and the N.Y.P.D is the family you don't want to mess with"

"I know that" I shot back.

"I don't think you do. You see this ain't the eighties where they take you to court to embarrass you nowadays they're coming to end your family tree and for them they'll have their family in the jury box. Look I have a favor to call in and I'll call it in for you; however you use it is up to you and your brother" my uncle made a call and begun speaking Russian, When he started that? I don't know but remembering who he was these might be some serious motherfuckers on the other end. James was rolling a blunt than some gorgeous dark skinned female walked in the room wearing a sexy see through lingerie James stopped what he was doing and said.

"Damn" looking at the woman my uncle laughed and said.

"Watch it boy that's my wife" my uncle sixty something and she had to be in her early thirties I just looked and said to my uncle.

"Um go ahead Unc."

"What her? Shit as long as he got blood in its veins than she can get plugged" he said smiling pointing at his manhood, he finished his call and we smoked like three blunts back to back my uncle took the team to his guest house and said.

"My favor will be coming though you all stay here handle your business here and don't worry about shit"

My uncle was always there for me every since my dad died he has never walked away, I looked at my twin and everybody else that came with us, I knew we was good cause when my uncle was dancing in this life, he wasn't to be fucked with but the times and people are different and knowing him he'll want to pick up his old toys I had a few messages from Amanda and Vasquez I listened to Amanda's.

"I need you or James to call a.s.a.p" I pushed the call button and she picked it right up.

"What's so important?"

"I was doing the checkup you asked me to do. Is James around you?" she asked sounding like she was up all night.

"Yeah why what's going on?" I put the phone on speaker

"There's a name that I heard James say that I've been seeing a lot of"

"What name is that?" James asked

When she said the name I could see the hurt in his eyes, the name she said was of his boy who he had put his trust in, the room has gotten quiet cause all m twin has ever done since we've gotten back all he done was spoken good of this guy now he finds not only was he close to the assholes we're after. He could be the reason his son has gotten his baby wings. I looked at m twin and said

"Look don't worry about it we're going to handle all these motherfuckers trust me on that" although he knew I wasn't lying I could see that was something he didn't want to hear which anyone can tell but what had threw me was his response.

"Okay so twin. How are we going to handle this situation" he said calmly, and no matter how bad I wanted to talk about it he was right we had a situation we had to handle and knowing my twin right now he was planning the niggaz death Bang came over and told my twin something that made him pay full attention.

"You know that I got family in the spot where your man is"

"Nah that's okay I got this one. I want everybody here on their shit cause this shits about to get lit" James said which was all true, whatever was to happen I'm sure that m bother knew how to handle it.

We stayed in my uncle's guest house that night making up a plan which was a good one, by the time we was done the sun was trying to sneak out. When I fully got up I haven't seen my twin

Chapter 28

Narrator

It's been a few days after the funeral of the twins mother was when the visits of the N.Y.P.D begin making their move.

Yani was riding though the streets of Lower Manhattan making a drop with two of James runners, and her partner Black, to her late night runs are always the best, while in the back of her car was five police cruisers was right on her trail as she drove unaware of her company coming up behind her, Black which sat in the passenger side seen the flashing lights.

"What's going on back there?" he asked Yani she looked and said

"Don't worry about them we're good. We haven't done shit yet"

As she continued to drive her heart jumped when she heard the words coming from behind her,

"You in the black Lexus Jeep pull over" Yani knew that she had at least 25 years of drugs in the car not including the guns, Yani looked over to Black and Dolly that was sitting in the back seat with Breezy, a young hot head that loves to see other individuals blood and said.

"What you guys want to do? We're fucked if we stop and dead if we don't so what it's going to be?" Yani asked already knowing what her next move should be she reached in the little hideaway in the driver's side door and displayed a black semi automatic she passed it to Black and said with an evil smile.

"Let's get the fuck out of here! Let's make those motherfuckers hate their jobs"

3 days prior.

Vasquez was in the interrogation room handcuffed to the table he knew the routine because he has placed some of New York's worst motherfuckers in this same place, he knew where this was going, he had to be sitting in that spot waiting for his life to come to an end for maybe two hours already.

The door had opened and two plain clothes officers walked in the room looking like they just wanted to lock somebody anybody up, and here was Vasquez, one of the officers was a tall mid chocolate complexion he looked like he could pass for Jamie Fox bother, he was dressed a little too sharp to be working it looked like they tried to be the bad niggaz of the streets, one of the officers was carrying a box of papers while the other held a legal folder they both sat across from Vasquez placing pictures and other looking evidence on top of the table allowing him to see that he was fucked.

"So Mr. Vas I'm federal officer White and this is my partner but you don't need to worry.."

"Look why the fuck am I here?" Vasquez asked already knowing the answer.

"Let's not play this game Vas we got you but the thing is if you want to be alone on this ride. However you look at it you're done, so why don't you just bring a little company with you"

Vasquez looked at everything that was displayed on top of the table officer White looked at his partner than at Vasquez and said

"You know you can call your delegate right?"

"I haven't done shit. So no I won't be calling her." Vasquez said not knowing everything that was in the box.

"Okay, I tried helping you see I do believe that there's still a cop, you know one of the good guys somewhere in there. I know you know what you have to do. Look the officer that was making the case wasn't a dumb guy." He said taking out some pictures and sliding them over to Vasquez "So I think you ought to think about that one with you saying that you haven't done shit."

The two federal officers had left the room leaving Vasquez to watch the photos, when he looked at the photo it was of him and two of Nora and James people looked to be burying something or one and as he kept looking it just go more worse for him he begun to sweat and placed his head in his hands and now started to worry, the doors opened and Davenport walked in he gave Vasquez a look and asked.

"So is all this worth it? You are throwing your life away for those two murdering fucks. Or are you going to be a man for once? Mike died from their hands or you don't care about that"

Vasquez thought about his options and where his future is heading he was about to say something but stopped when the door opened and entered federal officer White and his partner walked in Davenport shook his head and walked out

"So officer.. Well can we call you that?" he said sarcastically Vasquez knew if he'll talk he was good being dead so he just gave them someone close.

"Look I don't know what you want to know but I can say what I do know" Vasquez took a deep breath White took out a recorder and that's when Vasquez stared telling them about a drop that suppose to be happening in Harlem then said

"Now I would like my delegate please?" the two federal officers gave each other a look than walked out, Vasquez knew his time was on borrowed time which was getting real short.

3 ½ weeks prior

Lisa has been waiting in the precinct ready to help solve her uncle's murder, she was about to leave until she heard the voice from the earlier phone call

"Would you like this?" when she looked up Davenport stood there with two hot cups in his hand she took one of the cups and the officer said "I'm Officer Eric. Davenport I thank you for waiting" he and the young teen went to an empty interrogation room that he knew his partner would use, as the two entered the room Davenport seen his promotion coming out of his fifteen years being on the force he has never been close to any other Officer as he was to Mike so he had something to do and dead or alive those two twins was going the fuck down. He sat the girl down than sat across from her he looked at her and said

"Look if this is too hard we.."

"No,, I'm.. I'm okay" she bent her head and when she opened her mouth Davenport was so happy of what she was saying then she said something giving him a paper

"The morning he had died or rather gotten murdered he had left me that, and not only that he also told me if anything was to ever happen to him to quickly contact you and let you know that he was with that guy James that morning and I know that he was the one please don't let him get away bad enough he's still walking around. Him and that bitch twin of his" Davenport had stood up and walked over to where she sat and said kneeling down

"I swear to you those two and everybody behind them starting with Vasquez will be all going down" she looked at Davenport in the eyes and said with fear

"But there's something you need to know about these two that my uncle had told me these two aren't your normal street hustlers their worst than Satan himself. You'll need everybody and thing with you" Davenport haven't said anything he just nodded his head, he never been the type of guy who would look war in the face and be scared he was ready for what was to ever come his way. (So he thought) Davenport exited the room, while the young teen sat she begun talking to herself or rather thinking out loud, she waited for Davenport to return for five minutes and when he returned he was accompanied by a women police Officer

"Will you do me a favor and give this young lady a lift Ms. Young?" Davenport asked

"No problem but you owe me" she shot back at him

2 days later..

As soon as the four brothers stepped off the plane on U.S soil they looked like they didn't belong they youngest of the four took out the car key button they has gotten from the mail the day before when they found the car it was a cherry red Cherokee they all got in the car and drove to Queens the driver took out his phone and gave it to his brother and said in his Russian tongue

"Call him let him know we here"

The four brothers knew that since they've been called it's no doubt that somebody had the wrong but right kind of problems, the phone had rung once and he said

"My zdes" he said to whom he was speaking to.

"Priyekhat' v kvins" was said in their own tongue then both hung up the phone when he told of their destination no matter what they wanted to do in between they knew they came for business.

Before reaching their location they had to stop at the postal Derek was a very cautious man, years as runner, him and his boys ran New York for years he did a little tore in the army Derek had his hand in everything criminal and has never spent a day in jail his motto was plain and simple if a man is going to play a game just to lose there's no sense in that game being played and most of his boys had thought the same.

The Russian had reached one of the three postal offices they usually use when they come to America two of the brothers walked in and went to separate boxes opened them and took out the contents one had a briefcase full of money and the other had all the guns the needed for their job.

Present.

Yani had came to a sharp stop, she looked at all that was now in the car and asked that one question.

"Is everybody ready to get out this bullshit?" she took her two glocks out of their holsters she knew it was only one way out of this well really two but she only seen one.

"You in the black Cherokee turn off your engines and step out of the car" they heard coming from behind them everybody else that was in the car also done the same as Yani Black opened the passenger side door then the two back doors opened then the driver side all with their guns ready same as the police both sides ready to let their sides be seen as the strongest Dolly stepped out already knowing her fate she had her hands up waiting until Black made his move Breezy also stepped out holding his gun Yani done the same all ready for Black's move and once it was made that's when both sides opened fire while hiding behind the parked cars Dolly and Breezy held each other while Yani and Black done the same Yani kneeling in front of the car while bullets pierced through the body and windows of her week new Cherokee she asked with a smile

"Bet you didn't see this one happening today huh?"

"Well they're playing our shit. Let's go dance" Dolly and Breezy gave each other a hug and they both said fuck it and done what they always do at play time. Dolly and Breezy both stood up and started shooting back both knew they wasn't getting out of this alive they both shooting while bullets pierced though their body once the two dropped and their fight was over.

Yani was ready for this but what she didn't know was how the fuck have they could've known where they were going Yani has taken this drive for years and never been approached now she has to shoot her way out of this she looked at Black and said

"Somebody is working against us"

"What?"

"Somebody had to have said something. I never been fucked with coming this way" when she was done she took a look from where they hid and seen the worst thing she could've seen her two friends was getting shot down by the N.Y.P.D than they heard coming from the cops

"Look as you can see there's nowhere to go, you can either be smart come out so we can go home or you can act like Dumb and Dumber over here. You have ten seconds or we coming after you two" the guy started counting down from ten Black looked at Yani and gave her a passionate kiss and said.

"If I have to die I'm okay that it's with you" they both counted to three and done what they loved doing not letting their fear nor emotions get the best of them they tried taking as much of them that they can bring on the ride with them Black shot from top and Yani took the bottom the more they shot the more cops came as they bullets has gotten low the two done all they could've done and that's tried getting away which didn't happen as soon as they started to run bullets begun piercing through their flesh as the two begun to fall the last thing they've could've seen was the police moving in before they seen darkness.

Chapter 29

Bang

This shit had hit the fan after my boys moms funeral, it was also fucked up that Bags had got into a car accident that same night their moms had died that was fucked up on us all, James and Nora uncles people came down from Russia and had the time of their lives knocking off that nigga Noah's family they had killed everybody down to the dogs, Nora and James had me to speak to my boy to deal with that Blue motherfucker, now we had to deal with these cop motherfuckers, Vasquez had gotten locked up and right then and there we knew that shit was about to get different real quick, We was all at Greenwich Hospital with teddy bears, balloons, flowers, and all while James wife was giving birth to their son, it was a few of us all around every exit and stairway, but I didn't like this feeling that I was having like something real fucked up was about to happen, we was in the waiting room when Nora came out with a smile on her face and said to everybody who could hear.

"My nephew is here!! And he's a cutie"

We've been trying to contact some of our people with no luck Boe came in the hospital looking like he was just running for his life and what looked to be a shot in his arm

"Yo blood what the fuck!" came from the back from one of our people

"They..th.. They got Yani and Black" he shot back when Nora heard that; that quickly caught her full attention.

"Who the fuck gotten Yani? What the fuck are you talking about?" Nora asked

"Blaze had sent us to make a drop next thing you know them damn fucking pigs was coming at us"

"So what the fuck happen to Yani?"

"She's gone boss, her, Black Dolly and Breezy is all dead now" Nora rushed to the back she came back like three minutes later with James and by the look on his face this beautiful night was about to get real ugly James walked over to Boe and walked him over to the corner sat him down and the two of them had started speaking.

I looked at everybody who was in the room and those who wasn't here was counted for band right there I knew what went down and I knew for a doubt that they was on their way, I searched my side to see if I had my bad bitch with me. Since I've been around the team I hadn't had to be in but one shootout now that we had this police shit on our backs.. I had stopped them from talking and had told them what I had thought, I knew what they was talking about and I knew how James felt about Black when I reached over to where they sat it felt real cold and not by the temperature James looked like he wanted everybody without the same blood as him dead, I've gotten close and said.

"James can I have a word?" I asked

"What's up? And make it fast" he shot back

"It was your boy the cop" I said

"What the fuck are you talking about?"

"Vasquez, he had to say something"

"I know, we going to take care of this just like we take care of every other little problem"

James stood up and went back to his family, before getting back he looked back and said

"Get back to work" than he went behind the swinging doors, I didn't know why but my insides was acting up and my kill finger was itching a few of us had left I had stayed back this war we had wasn't no we can plan the shit we just had to kill on sight, James and Nora was on family time Blaze was out of town handling business, I really hated hospitals I went outside to have a smoke I was glad for my boy not only did he have the family but he now had his own.

With all the shit that was going on Nora didn't want her nephew to stay in the hospital so some of the team was suppose to have taken Kiss and her new son out from the back, we couldn't take any chances, while I stood out front smoking something had caught my attention, although this was a hospital it was weird that this place was still packed I didn't feel right I took out my phone and called James but guess he was too caught up to pick up as I stood outside the scene didn't look too much like an hospital scene I called Nora the phone rang twice as soon as I heard her voice I heard the metallic click of a gun followed by.

"If you move you die" I pressed for the speaker hoping that they'll hear what's going on. With my hands still up I said.

"What's going on? What the fuck is this?" already knowing the answer I knew if they was to get in this place James and Nora was good as locked up, while the shine of their lights hitting me in the face I said a silent prayer than said fuck it, I quickly went for my guns with no chance as soon as I reached that's when they let their shots off.

Narrator;

Bang was outside smoking a cigarette, all night he felt something was off and he was now about to see that the feeling was right. As he walked further he begun looking in all the individuals that was around bang tried calling James but couldn't catch him so he just continued his thinking his gut was bothering him so he had called Nora the phone rang twice as soon as she picked up Bang heard behind him a metallic sound of a gun followed by.

"If you move you die" Bang had the phone on speaker hoping that Nora heard what was happening, when Bang turned to face who was behind him,

"What the fuck is this about?" Bang asked trying to figure a way out which was none he knew that who they wanted was now upstairs but what he didn't know is, how long were they here for? Bang knew that if they had gotten upstairs James Nora and Kiss was easy as locked up or dead, he said a silent prayer and said fuck it he went for his guns causing the police to open fire on him before he could've gotten hold of his guns he was shot up dropping to the floor the N.Y.P.D had moved in.

Inside the hospital the shots that was fired was heard running everywhere the commotion had caused a diversion hearing what just happened Nora, James, Kiss and their new son John was able to sneak through the back.

Meeting up with the little of their team that stayed back they've reached the parking lot quickly getting to their cars they hurried in and quickly pulled off

Chapter 30

James

I couldn't believe it this night has finally arrived my son was being born, my wife went into labor and I was nervous but ready I took my wife and rushed her to our Cherokee I called my sister and told her where to meet me my wife was screaming in pain sitting in the passenger side I looked at her and said trying to cheer her up

"Baby you got this, remember we. Well you done this already" although I didn't see it I felt her staring a hole in my face.

One thing I hated about these rainy nights is the way the roads feel as we drive I seen the lights to the hospital right ahead, it was like the closer we got the harder her pain felt shit was scaring the fuck out of me but I was also happy a second chance at becoming a father and then it came back to me that I wasn't there to protect them the first time, as the hospital got closer so did my fear now that we have problems with the fucking N.Y.P.D damn why the fuck have I done that bullshit now here I am about to have a baby and these motherfuckers want to take me to be with my dad I called my twin when she picked up I said.

"Yo call the team and have motherfuckers meet us at the hospital"

"Already done" she said

"Where you're at?" I asked

Once we reached the hospital I rushed my wife inside and quickly made a scene I didn't give a fuck about nobody else's problems or shit. The nurses came and took my wife and put her in a wheelchair and took her to the delivery room I followed behind ready for the arrival of my prince.

When my twin showed up she was accompanied with at least 30 of our peoples not everybody but most had balloons and teddy bears, and I also knew they all had their heat on them.

"Damn did you bring enough motherfuckers with you?" I asked

"I rather live to see tomorrow instead of dying today. My work is not done. Besides; I don't trust any of those P.D assholes" she said

Twin and I went to the delivery room to be with my wife, we've gotten covered up and entered the room my wife was laying there ready to become a mother I looked at how beautiful she was and said.

"How's my queen?" I asked

"You're ready for this girl?" twin asked

She had screamed and that's when the doctors done their jobs.

It took them five hours and the world was introduced to my son when it was over my sister ran out the delivery room with a huge smile on her face I looked down at my wife smiled and gave her a kiss and said.

"I promise to always be there for the both of you. Thank you baby I love you" I stayed back with my wife and watched as she rest, a few minutes later I went down to join the team where there was half the team in the waiting area my twin was there having a laugh then out of nowhere Boe walked in holding his arm from which appeared to be a bullet wound he started telling us about what happened and right then and there I knew who it had to be, I took Boe to the corner to see what he could fill us in on Boe and myself had to be talking for no less than three minutes when Bang came over and tried telling me what I already knew Vasquez had to be talking I had told everybody to leave and go continue getting our money, I went back to my wife and child and my twin was also with me she said.

"I don't think that it would be wise if you keep the baby here"

"I'm not; but what I will do is make sure my son is good before he go home" while I was talking my phone was going off I checked and it was Bang I didn't want to hear shit about Vasquez so I just let my VM get it"

We got to my wife's room and she was still resting I walked in her room and kissed her awake, twins phone began ringing and when she answered she spoke for a sec than put it on speaker and we heard Bang saying.

"What the fuck is this about?"we heard him say than we heard police and seconds later we heard shots I looked over at my twin quickly took my son out of his mother's arms wrapped him up well and we all had left through the back where we was met by the rest of our team I gave my son and wife to one of the girls that came with us and said.

"Take them to my Uncles place in Queens we'll meet up later" I than looked at my twin and said with a smile "Time to let them know who they real bosses are huh?"

We got to the parking lot and jumped in our cars and pulled off I was with my twin in her car while my wife took my Cherokee the only thing that's been running through my head was how the fuck did they know where we was, I called Blaze and informed him in on what's going on he told me him and the crew was on their way.

"I guess that time has arrived huh?" twin asked

"I don't think that was the whole force; but what I need to know is who the fuck else is talking on our team. There was no way those motherfuckers was suppose to have been there"

I had sped up my drive Nora had hired a team of hit-men ready to kill and die for her she was on the phone telling them to meet at Chelsea Pier, she had a plan for this timing and also a getaway she was cautious as well as I am she bought out an old apartment building where everybody could hide out we also had to hide our funds Blaze and Keima took care of all of our products making sure that we had a good stash, she purchased it after Vasquez got knocked so we could lay up until we're ready to put all those blue shirts their retirement plan in motion.

We reached New York and drove to 23rd Street and Hudson being that it was late traffic was light we got to Chelsea quick and seen Keima leaning on her midnight blue Ford Explora her front lights was on and when she noticed twins car she stood up twin stopped right in front of her we both stepped out.

"Everybody's inside" Keima said

"And Blaze?" Nora asked

"He's on the third floor"

Twin, Keima and I walked inside of the building and went to the back where the team was waiting Nora called Blaze and told him to meet us in the back. The team was in back waiting on my twin and myself, once Blaze joined I began.

"Tonight was a good night for me and my wife but somebody here is Takashi 69ing" I said

"Boss what you're talking about?" came from the back

"Somebody is talking out here. That's what he's talking about" Nora said right when I was going to say something my heart had skipped a few beats when we heard from outside along with see flashing lights.

"Hello Nora and James Lee this is Officer Davenport the place is surrounded so it's best that you come out, with your hands up, or we're coming in" the asshole said.

Twin and I weren't stupid when she bought this building we put bullet proof widows we had two getaways I looked at my twin than at the team and said.

"I know what I'm saying and when I find out who you are you're dead. Now let's go give them hell"

We all went to every floor went and covered all the windows roof tops, and exits everybody took their post Blaze, twin, and myself had a doorway built in one of the apartments I heard the shooting from both sides I kept my twin close to me all I was thinking was I'm not losing her again. Now I knew somebody else was talking other than Vasquez I looked at my twin and said.

"We have to get out of here. Shits about to get heavy"

"I know, c'mon" we went to one of the apartments on the second floor it was a big banging sound coming from the front I looked out the window and seen these niggaz was trying everything to get inside of the building.

"Boy c'mon" twin said walking in the apartment.

Twin opened the hideaway and we walked in the hidden closet, while we walked I heard the commotion downstairs,

"Hurry the fuck up" I said

Twin was in front, I was second and Blaze was behind me we walked through the adjourning apartment and quickly rushed to the parking lot, we jumped in the two cars we had parked and pulled off, while driving off I noticed some of my people was laying on the floor the police found their way in I looked and shook my head in disbelief I looked at my twin and said.

"This won't be over unless we put this shit to rest"

"What you think?" she asked

"Bring it to them straight"

"With who Just the three of us?"

She was right we couldn't go back until we rebuild, but then again I started thinking about who I have in my life so I said.

"You want to call this a lost than?" I asked

"For now yeah, we'll get that back besides we have our work and our bread so everything's good"

Chapter 31

Narrator

It's been weeks since the twins was able to elude the police, unlike the rest of the Scorpion Sting contiguous was either dead or now on Rikers Island waiting on their day, Nora sent her girl Tia on that run to pick up her shit, Tia was one of the few that never been in the out she always played the back so she was the best pick for the job.

James and Nora was well known through the West just as well as the East all they had to do was show their faces and things went their way, she thought about her brother and also had thoughts of calling him but didn't know if their phones was bugged, and with every corner with video she didn't need her face being on everybody's T.V and phones she was very cautious of how she made her money Nora was smart beyond her years so making money wasn't nothing to her the one thing that roamed her mind was her nephew she knew her twin was good but what she didn't know was if he was still a free boss, the twins had a great run and would've still been having that run if it wasn't for a close hand of theirs Nora was sitting on her throne thinking about what the fuck went wrong and how the hell she couldn't see the snake that her right hand was

James was making a run for his family when a pair of young frighten eyes was planted on him while he walked out the grocery carrying bags for his wife, at first he was reluctant on going out but never saying no to his wife he went. The young girl from his pass seen him, she was with her young wannabe a man boyfriend whom promised to always protect her he seen the fear in her eyes as he asked, with his new 9mm under polo button up shirt he worn. The last time he seen this look on her face she an out the house like she saw her Aunt.

"What's the problem babe?" he asked.

"There he is over there. That's him the guy who was looking for me. Him and his sister" she answered darting a nervous finger at the handsome fellow walking to his black Benz the guy walked over to his car placing his bags in the backseat not knowing or even caring to look over his shoulders James continued his day.

Lisa and her young boyfriend walked their way over to the guy unaware of the two sneaking behind him pushing pass the people that was walking, once he was close enough the young man who has never shot a gun has casually went for his gun the young man placed his 9mm to back of James head and without another thought he fired (blam) not waiting another second to know if his shot has made its mark the young couple ran off leaving James bloody body laying on the side of his car now wondering what was going to happen next, there was a large crowd swarming around the wounded bloody body of one of the New York evil twins.

Two Weeks later :

In Miami Nora was starting to build a new empire she wanted her twin by her side she said fuck it and called her twin just to get a ringing phone Nora was on the balcony of the hotel she was staying in looking down at the lovely scenery, when Blaze walked in with his phone in hand, his look told Nora that this wasn't a friendly call placing the shaking I-phone to her ear she said.

"Talk" Nora was waiting to hear from her twin and out of all the news she was preparing herself for this wasn't one of the news she wanted to hear.

"He's in the hospital, your uncle has him hiding people think he's dead but he's not." came from the other end of the call

"First of all who the fuck is this" Nora yelled.

"It's Samantha, well Kiss they tried to kill my baby"

Nora stopped listening to what she was now hearing her twin best friend partner in crime is now in the hospital and she didn't know how bad was he, she was just about to get dressed when there was a knock at her door she called for Blaze but he wasn't nowhere to be found putting her robe on she went to answer the door and when she opened it her heart fell to what and who she saw standing there with guns aimed at her face.

"Ms. Lee can you place your hands where we.." she knew this speech she heard it being said to people for a long time but never thought the words was ever going to be said to her she closed her eyes knowing her run has just came to a stop she allowed the police to place a pair of handcuffs on her as they escorted Nora out not letting her get dressed she felt disrespected the police walked Nora out of the hotel when she stepped out she noticed that these people was the same as those New York motherfuckers she thought. Nora eye scanned the area and couldn't believe what she was looking at Blaze standing across the street smoking a cigarette the two eyes was met and Nora could've sworn she seen a smile on his face. Sitting in the back of the patrol car she asked.

"Why the fuck am I in your car?" she asked just to get ignored, Nora has always been cautious she's only shown her face when necessary so she knew they didn't had shit on her and if they did have anything on her it would be something she could get out of.

New York

Every since she has gotten the news Kiss has been in the home she shared with James crying in the bed. Her son was now also showing that he had a set of lungs also, out of everybody that's been in Kiss life is either dead or in jail before his death James has shown a lot of his team that he's a boss and bailed at least twenty of his team out Kiss has gotten out of the bed and went to her child she picked up her son and said to him.

"No matter what, I'm going to find out who tried taken your dad from us"

Kiss world has came to hell but just like any other time in her life Kiss was a fighter, money was now not a problem for her since her main family was bosses but her question to herself was Could she be labeled the same her help Ruth came in the room carrying her phone

"Ma'am the phone"

"Who is it?" Kiss said taking the phone

"Yes" she responded to who she was speaking to

"This is Nora I don't have a lot of time but if Blaze come see you don't trust him he called the police on me yesterday"

After the two women hung up Kiss went back to what she was doing she looked down at her son smiled the first time since she's gotten the news about her husband which she forgotten to tell Nora the news moving around in her room holding her child Kiss had a lot to think about and now she knew what she had to do not only have her king has almost been taken away from her; but she just found out that the strongest sister that she knew is now locked up Kiss knew she had to make a smart decision and looking down at her prince she knew what that decision had to be, she looked down at her prince and left him a strong promise

"I swear to you lil man mommy will always be here for you that I promise you"

Miami

He was sitting in his hotel room thinking to himself what the fuck has he just done to his life. For years Nora has ran New York and she was doing that alone but now she had a twin and Blaze knew if James was to get message of what he has done he was easily known as a dead man Blaze took out his phone and called his cousin who was still in New York trying to become a big man in the City.

"Talk to your boy cuzzo" than he said "Yo did you guys hear the news?"

"Nah, what's up?" Blaze asked

"It's all over out here your boy got popped"

"What? Who got popped?" Blaze asked acting like he didn't know what the News was.

"The twin, it's been said people seen two young kids running away from the shooting" Blaze was sort of relieved by the news, he told his family "Yo I have a huge supply of their shit over here." He said walking aound the room, than he continued. "The City is now ours boy" Blaze was proud of his actions unaware that Nora was now walking out the precinct thanks to her high paying lawyers Blaze took his chances and left the apartment, he was on his way to their storage not knowing that Nora and her lawyers was on their way as well Nora wasn't even upset at Blaze she knew that there's always going to be the close ones to you that would take you down, her lawyers and herself has gotten in the white Bentley that's been parked outside of the precinct the four jumped in the car and quickly pulled off the driver asked looking in the rearview.

"Where do you need to go boss?"

"Take me to my storage" Nora said putting on the clothes her lawyer has brought to her.

Once they've reached Miami Shores and drove to the safeguard storage Nora told everybody that's been in the car to wait and went to retrieve her product she took the two grey Nike duffle bags and went inside the storage, she stopped at the desk and told the sister behind the counter to give her the black 357 revolver, once she has gotten it Nora went to her locker and noticed that it was being occupied, without another thought she drawn her gun she lifted the gate and seen who was in her locker and seen Blaze trying to get her work, Nora cocked her gun and said before ending his life.

"You motherfucker, you tried to send me to jail and now you're trying to steal from me. You see there's always going to be that one mother fucker in every family that has that one stupid asshole but the shit that got me fucked up is that stupid mother fucker had to be you." Nora said with her gun aimed at his face.

Blaze knew his future was now coming to an abrupt ending before pulling the trigger she left him with something to take to hell with him

"You know how I am and you know that I don't like rats you see you're lucky my twin isn't around but I tell you what I'm going to let you live but.." she said shooting both of his legs once Blaze fell to the floor Nora kneeled down to face level and said "This will be your new home, I have to go back home. The Boss is back."

In pain Blaze had mustered the worst news Nora has ever heard

"Well boss you're going to have to do it alone cause James is no more he's dead" he said laughing at the hurt look in her eyes Nora couldn't hold back she just said fuck it and took his life after getting her shit out she locked the storage locker and left

"Here you go" she said giving the keys back "I'm done with this storage your business was great. And I need you to call Jake and make him clean the locker, nobody else but Jake"

"Thank you so much Ms. Lee. I'll get to that real soon" after giving back the gun she left out after leaving the clerk with a great amount of cash and left after putting her work and the cash they've also had hidden in the trunk she jumped in the car and told the driver

"Take me back to New York. They need to know the Boss is back"

Epilogue

Nora has gotten back to the City, her first stop was to her twin's wife which she found out that Kiss wasn't in her right state of mind. Once the two lady's was calm enough Nora and Kiss has went to get pay back for James being in the critical state he was now in, the two women been on the search for three days Nora decided to put whomever it was who tried to kill her twin in a deep rest before bringing her empire back up, her name and reputation was A+ all over and she had nothing but respect from all hustlers everywhere, she was a queen and she proved it every second of the day.

Once the two ladies seen their mark Nora and Kiss took the two to a warehouse in Brooklyn Nora didn't want this to go too long and she put a hole in the both of their heads, leaving the two dead bodies where they were the two ladies left. Nora than called the remaining shooters and runners that have been left of her team. Nora and Kiss was now two of the strongest women in New York being that James was recovering Kiss and Nora ran the City with an iron fist which was shown from day break too day end, Nora felt lost without her twin by her side but she never let it be seen, she built her empire up again more stronger than before she was sometimes the one who would let people slide but not this time around she and Kiss had no kind of care this City was theirs and they was willing to show anybody who thought differently.

Nora wanted to lay low first until the snitch would've came out but once she found out who it was she knew it was time to go back home Kiss and Nora was on a rampage in the streets of New York nobody was safe and everybody was money Kiss kept her son close to her she trusted no one with her child every time she looked down at her prince she seen her husband face Nora's team was ruthless whatever problems they've had in the pass Nora made sure that it was taken care of, but no matter who was around them or how trusting they would be Nora missed her twin, after the funeral she Kiss and the rest of her team went out looking for Lisa and her lil boyfriend the search only took three days and when they were found Nora had showed the both of them why she and James was the twin bosses of New York.

1 Year Later:

Nora made sure that every one of her soldiers that had fell she made sure that each one of their families was taken care of, Kiss opened a nonprofit program for the kids but that was only for their money, Nora had a new team for each of her establishments she had to be more ruthless than before being that James backed away for a little while, and since Boe, Bang, Yani, Black and Mells all the individuals she trusted was gone Nora and James was most defiantly the twin bosses of New York and Kiss and Nora made sure that they names would been remembered dead or alive.

The

End

9 781952 155789